HOMELESS WITH SIX DOGS

Homeless with Six Dogs
And Other Stories

A collection of short stories
by

SEVASTI IYAMA

Adelaide Books
New York / Lisbon
2020

HOMELESS WITH SIX DOGS

And Other Stories

A collection of short stories

By Sevasti Iyama

Published by Adelaide Books, New York / Lisbon
adelaidebooks.org

Editor-in-Chief
Stevan V. Nikolic

For any information, please address Adelaide Books
at info@adelaidebooks.org

or write to:

Adelaide Books
244 Fifth Ave. Suite D27
New York, NY, 10001

ISBN: 978-1-951896-33-1

Printed in the United States of America

For Jason and Zoe

Contents

The Poor Widow ***9***

Where is Buddha? ***15***

The Madwoman of Wigs ***27***

The Locket ***35***

Odin ***46***

Funeral Preparations for Mr. Cromwell D. Scone, God Rest His Soul ***70***

A Winter Coat ***72***

Bel Air, 2500 ***78***

Homeless with Six Dogs ***81***

Welcome to Trona ***91***

Jellyfish ***101***

Desperately seeking Xanax Due to Severe Anxiety As Inflicted by Yucca Brevifolia ***107***

Angie **120**

The Holy Face Medal **129**

Help Wanted: Live In Nanny.
Free Room and Board. One West 72nd Street. **140**

About the Author **149**

The Poor Widow

As she perched on the edge of a white loveseat like a sparrow on a tree branch, Kate Nigoshito squinted as she flipped through the pages of *The San Francisco Chronicle.*

Where were her glasses?

The plastic that covered the loveseat made a crinkly sound, much like the noise of the Saran Wrap that Kate used to cover take-out from Sushi Sam's, her favorite Japanese restaurant in San Francisco. Many years ago, Kate had been a beautiful woman. Now her face had a veil of bitterness. She looked like the Japanese version of Beth Jarrett as portrayed by Mary Tyler Moore from the film *Ordinary People.* Unlike Beth Jarrett, who left her husband at the end of the film, Kate had been a loving and loyal wife to Toshiro. For fifty years, two months, one day, three hours, fifteen minutes and ten seconds, she stood by Toshiro's side, or Tosh. When the DOW soared like a kite, they celebrated by driving the Ferrari up to NAPA, where they drank Shiraz, ate oysters and Brie and danced to Frankie Valli and the Four Seasons. When the stock market crashed, back in 1987, they clung to each other and wept like Hansel and Gretel lost in the forest.

Twenty years ago, Tosh designed the austere Bank of America building in Oakland, along with other business buildings in the Bay Area. He had conceived their Modern Greek style house in Piedmont. The home had a Japanese garden, complete with a waterfall.

What a brilliant architect Tosh had been! What a wonderful and loving husband! Where was the stupid obituary?

As hard as she looked, she could not find the announcement. She definitely needed her glasses. She searched underneath the white loveseat, and behind the six-foot tall Bonsai tree. Then, she tackled the area behind the exquisite black Japanese folding screen that depicted cherry blossoms, and a smiling geisha waving a fan. As Kate scoured the living room, she waved her hands about. The smoke that wafted from jasmine incense positioned in front of the Butsudan permeated her nostrils. She and Tosh had picked up the exquisite Buddhist altar on their honeymoon in Tokyo. Now the altar occupied half of the Chinese rosewood flower carving round dining tabletop. While she brandished her hands in the air, waving away smoke, she resembled Vladimir Horowitz conducting Beethoven's *Fifth Symphony*. Suddenly, she halted.

"I am just a poor widow," she said, sobbing. "A poor widow."

One day, her obituary would appear in *The San Francisco Chronicle*. After all, she was almost seventy, and Tosh was seventy-two years of age when he passed away a week ago. When the doctor had asked her if she wanted to remove Tosh from life support, she did not hesitate. Why should she let her beloved husband suffer? When her time came, she did not want to agonize! Ah, how she wanted to rid herself of these morbid thoughts! She grabbed a Kleenex from the coffee table and blew her nose. Besides the Kleenex, there was a beautiful Japanese vase filled with lilies. She had purchased the vase from an antique store. These days, she needed all the comfort that she could get. Next to the glass, was a porcelain white bottle full of saké. She poured herself a cup. She needed to pamper herself.

Luckily, she was going on a trip to Japan soon. Being in the company of other grieving widows and widowers would surely provide comfort. Staying at the Peninsula Tokyo would be soothing. Or perhaps, she should stay at the Imperial Hotel so that she could save money. However, that was a ridiculous idea. The Japanese American Widower, or Widow (depending on the sex of the bereaved) Society had booked a floor at the Peninsula. Staying at the Imperial, while the rest of JAWS stayed at the Peninsula, was an inconsiderate and rude idea.

After fifteen minutes of searching aimlessly, she spotted the Cartier glasses behind the altar. Inside the Butsudan was a golden statue of the Amida Buddha along with an exquisite golden gong and wooden mallet. Next to the gong, was a framed eight by ten photograph of Tosh, wearing Givenchy and Gucci, standing in front of his black Testa Rossa Ferrari. Her newly dead husband stared straight at the camera lens, with a humble smile, and thumbs up. Right next to the framed photo, was a white ivory bowl, full of distilled water. A cherry blossom floated on top of the water. Next to the bowl, was a crystal glass brimming with Shiraz, his favorite wine, along with a black bowl containing two oranges, three Fuji apples, a California roll and a pop tart.

Reluctantly, she lit the jasmine incense. She was allergic to incense, but it was only fitting that she honor her beloved dead spouse.

After she placed her glasses on her nose, she rotated her head, like a submarine periscope searching for an enemy. Where had she put the newspaper? Perhaps her sorrow was causing her to lose her mind. Maybe she should make two steaming hot cups of green tea. One cup would be for her, to perk up her spirits. Another cup would be for Tosh, of course.

As she headed for the kitchen, she heard the loud sound of the gong reverberate throughout the living room. Kate turned to see a spirit, wearing Hugo Boss, and Nike sneakers. She gasped. Her Cartier glasses fell off her nose and onto the floor. The apparition floated over to the loveseat, picked up the *Chronicle,* quickly skimmed through the pages, and then stared at Kate, grinning. It was the spirit of Tosh! Waving *The Chronicle*, he bobbed around the room like a rubber duck on the top of a bathtub.

"Kon'nichiwa," he said, with a hint of a Japanese accent. Even though they had lived in the states for years, he still considered Japanese his first language.

"Tosh?!?"

She felt as if she were about to faint. Then she quickly gathered her wits.

"Tosh? Beloved husband, is that really you?" she asked.

"If you had purchased a full page ad, you would have discovered the obituary of Tush Nigoshit much more quickly," said Tosh.

He hurled the newspaper back on the couch.

"Oh my dearest, the copy editor did not proofread your name," said Kate, before she sneezed. The syrupy smell of jasmine was killing her. She wanted to extinguish the incense, but the Tosh ghost was soaring above the altar. She could not bear to be within a foot of that thing.

"A pop tart?" asked Tosh.

"I am a poor widow, Tosh," said Kate.

"You can buy persimmons from Ralphs for a dollar a pound!" He floated to the window, where the blinds had been drawn shut. After the specter moved away from the window,

Kate ran over to the blinds, and pulled them open. Perhaps the light would cause the ghost to leave. The sun filled the room. While Kate blinked her eyes from the sunlight that practically blinded her, Tosh spun around the living room like a kite. He was very much present in the room and had no intention of leaving.

"How was my funeral?" asked Tosh, coming to a halt.

Why couldn't he just go back to the land of the dead and reincarnate? She thought, as she gripped the edge of the love-seat. She calmly said, "There were hundreds of people there, who came to say goodbye. Our broker, your business associates, family and of course, the Buddhist monk. First there was the viewing, then the ceremony, and finally the cremation. The monk delivered a beautiful speech. The funeral was peaceful albeit tragic. Oh! Per your request, your remains were placed inside the beautiful neoclassical monument that you designed. Inside the Chapel of the Chimes, of course."

"You wanted to save face," said Tosh.

"Well, what was I supposed to do, you moron? Put your ashes in a dust buster?" Kate tripped, and grabbed the sofa, before she fell flat on her face. As she pulled herself up, she saw that she had snagged her sheer knee-highs that she wore to keep the white rug spic and span. The specter stared at her with an evil smile. Then, the damn ghost began to waltz around the room. Why was it dancing? It was dead!

"Buddha say, you will not be punished for your anger, you will be punished by your anger," said Tosh, before he stopped dancing and curtsied.

"During your lifetime, the only church you attended was the Temple of Merrill Lynch!" Kate said.

Then, Tosh began to fade away.

"Where the hell are you going?" she asked.

Tosh became more transparent, to the point where he was almost invisible. She could barely make out his face.

"Too bad I died first," he sighed. "A trip with JAWS. What fun!"

Suddenly, it dawned on her. Perhaps she would see him in the next lifetime, or perhaps she wouldn't! And even if she did come upon him, they would be in different bodies. They might sense that they knew each other in a previous lifetime, but would not know that they had been husband and wife.

Even though the sun filled the room, she shivered.

"Do you want a cup of green tea?" she asked, hysterically.

"After one dies, there is a reincarnation sign up sheet. I must make sure that my next life will be favorable," he said, waving at her.

And then he was gone. Kate fell on her knees, and wept. After a minute, she got up to her feet. She slowly staggered to the window, and drew the blinds. Darkness filled the room. After she picked up the framed photograph of Tosh, she saw that the pop tart was gone.

Where is Buddha?

"Is Buddha okay?" she asks, as she sits up in the hospital bed. On top of her hospital tray table is a small container of 2% fat milk with a straw, a blueberry muffin still in its wrapper, and a plastic tray containing Salisbury steak, mashed potatoes, and corn. Since she arrived to the psych award, two days ago on a 5150, she has not eaten.

The nurse walks into the room with a tray holding a bunch of pills, all different colors, along with a small paper cup full of water.

It's time for her cocktail.

The nurse watches as she swallows all of the pills, and drinks the water.

After the nurse leaves, she says, "There's dry food in the kitchen, along with his water bowl. And he has a favorite squeaky toy. Make sure that's by his bed. He loves that toy. I hope he didn't chew up the walls. He has serious separation anxiety. Just tell him mommy will be home soon."

"He wouldn't let me in," I say.

"I gave you a key!" she says, panicking.

"I know a sober living home in Bakersfield that might be a great fit for you," I say.

She looks at me and says, "Doesn't stupid AA preach about goddamn honesty? What the fuck is wrong with you?"

"Please don't curse," I say.

"Where is Buddha?" she screams. "Where is my dog? What did you do with him?"

What was I supposed to do? Not only would the dog not let me past the front door, but also he tried to bite me. I called 911 to get help. After the cops and paramedics came to the dilapidated house on Fulop Street, north of Lake Isabella Boulevard, they could not get in either, so they called animal control, and they came and used a catchpole to try and snare him. Just as they almost snagged him, he bolted into the bedroom and guarded her as she lay on a fetal position on the floor. An animal control officer backed him into a corner, and caught him. As the dog was pulled out of the room, he whined and tried to bite the officer.

Finally, the paramedics were able to get to her. She was unconscious. There were empty bottles of Xanax, and vodka on the ground next to her body.If I hadn't gotten there in time, she would have died. But no, she was more concerned about crazy Buddha.

I muster up enough courage to say, "He is at the pound."

She grabs the tray of food and hurls it right into my face. Then she starts screaming like a lamb being slaughtered.

While the orderlies and a nurse shoot her up with Haldol and strap her to the bed, I march out the door. My face is covered with gravy and mashed potatoes. Somehow the corn and steak have ended up under my blouse. The steak is cold.

She has hardly any money and barely survives from student loans. She pursues her Masters in Creative Writing and writes short stories. Besides Buddha, writing keeps her alive, or so she says. I have often told her that she needs to get a practical job, because writing does not pay the bills, and now she is getting evicted, which is probably why she did what she did. Financial stress, let alone eviction, is traumatic, especially for a single woman who lives alone with an English bulldog pit bull mix. She hates Lake Isabella. The neighbors harass her. One girl calls her a bitch, because she keeps to herself. She believes that her eviction is not an example of God doing for us, what we can't do for ourselves. This is an illustration of God telling her to drop dead.

As I drive home, I smoke a Capri. She has just lost two years of sobriety. I don't think she can bear to get another newcomer chip.

When I first meet her at an AA meeting, her teeth are rattling like a pair of maracas. She has a fever, and is shaking uncontrollably. I tell her that she has DT's and needs to go to the hospital. She refuses, saying that she can't go to the hospital because she has no one to watch Buddha. Since I don't care much for dogs, I don't volunteer. Then, she says that her childhood sucked, and that life had always been hard, and the only thing she loves more than life itself is Buddha. She tells me all about her finding Buddha wandering around somewhere on Lake Isabella Boulevard. He was thirsty, weary and his ribs were as skeletal as those of a dinosaur on exhibit at the Museum of Natural History. Buddha did not have a collar let alone a microchip. Instead there was a tight rope around his neck, as if he had escaped execution by hanging. She also asks me if I can sponsor her. Like an idiot, I say yes. I buy her a Big Book.

A week later, we meet at Burger King to work the steps.

While she sullenly stares at page 59 of her Big Book, which looks like it has been used as a dog toy let alone a coaster, I ask, "Do you believe that you are powerless over alcohol and that your life is unmanageable?"

In response, she loudly slurps her vanilla ice coffee which I bought for her, of course, since she is broke.

"Do you believe that you are powerless over alcohol and that your life is unmanageable?" I repeat.

Instead of replying, she looks away, staring at the customers in line waiting for their orders. Some are overweight. After a minute, she stares at me with a look of disgust.

"Fat people ready to eat poor dead cows," she says. "They make me sick."

I drive by the Lake Isabella Shelter to see if it's open. The shelter is closed. From the outside, I hear dogs barking and crying. It is cold out. I head home.

I live in a nice mobile home in Wofford Heights. There are wind chimes hanging from my porch. My garden is pristine. There is a birdbath, birdhouses hanging from oak trees, and roses covered with plastic to protect them from the cold. As I walk up the steps to my front door, a wave of depression crosses over me. I get a sudden urge to go to the liquor story and buy a bottle of wine. For the first time, in six years, I desperately want to drink.

The next morning, I am at the shelter, trying to find the goddamn dog. It's a fairly small shelter, with only about twenty kennels. I see dogs, mainly pit bulls. A small matted terrier, shaking with terror, is curled up on an old baby blanket in a corner of his kennel. His eyes are closed. Next to him, a Siberian husky with piercing blue eyes claws at the bars. A senior

German shepherd patrols inside his kennel. His owners probably dumped him there, because he grew old. Even though he is in the pound, he tries to maintain his poise. But I can sense his despair. He is an old dog and probably won't make it out of there alive. And yet, despite his despair, he keeps his head held high. In the midst of chaos, he maintains the little dignity that he has left.

The rest of the kennels contain pit bulls. A red nosed pit bull, along with three other pit bulls, stand in a corner of their kennels as if they know that no one is coming for them. They have looks of defeat. Their spirit is gone.

Suddenly, I see an English bulldog pit bull mix that appears calm in the midst of insanity. He is as still as a lotus plant. There is a paper inside a plastic sleeve posted on the outside of his kennel. An identification number A456789, is right underneath his name, Buddha. Both the number and his name are written in heavy black magic marker. *Owner surrender* is written in pen underneath A456789.

"Owner surrender," the officer says, as if I am an idiot who can't read.

"That's impossible. She never surrendered the dog."

"Well, someone did," she says.

"I'd like to adopt him," I say.

"Dog's not available until tomorrow at nine," she says.

"I will be here tomorrow," I say.

"Be here on time. Vet's also coming at nine, and then we have to empty out cages. Make room for other arrivals. No telling if he will be here or not if you are late."

"That doesn't make sense," I say. "He's available at nine, but he might be euthanized at nine?"

"Pit bulls are a dime a dozen," she says.

"But he's a pit bull mix!" I say.

"Most of them are," she says.

I stare at the cages. Staring at me, some of the dogs bark frantically. They are all begging me to help them, get them out of there and take them home. Some are young, others old, but all of them have lives that are at someone else's mercy.

Buddha is quiet. His eyes are closed, as if he is meditating. If he can speak, I can almost hear him chant, "Nam-myoho-renge-kyo."

The animal control officer has artificial purple and white plastic nails. How the hell can she work with dogs with those talons? She eyes me staring at her fingers.

"I like your nails," I lie.

Why the hell did I just say that? Jesus. Twenty years sober and I am still a people pleaser. Talk about character defects.The officer does not respond.

I take a deep breath.

"I'll be here at 8:45," I say.

Even though I have a hold on the dog, I do not trust the animal control officer with the artificial purple and white claws. I am nervous. After I leave the shelter, I drive on the 178 East past Paradise Cove, a picturesque campsite that overlooks the lake. On the opposite side of the freeway, is the Paradise Inn motel and steakhouse restaurant. I ate prime rib there once, but now the idea makes me ill to my stomach. After she mentioned dead cows at Burger King, my stomach curdles when I think of meat.

She loves to go to Kissack Bay, which looks out over the lake. There are trails there. For the most part, Kissack Bay tends to be isolated. She is a loner, so the place suits her to a tee. When she runs with Buddha at Kissack Bay, she listens to depressing grunge music on Pandora. She loves Soundgarden. Her favorite Soundgarden song is *Fell on Black Days*.

The song begins to play in my head.

"Whatsoever I've feared has come to life, Whatsoever I've fought off became my life ..."

I drive into Kissack bay and park close to the lake. There is a crescent moon, which casts an unearthly glow. I get out of my car, and walk.

It's icy cold and windy. I give up trying to light a cigarette, and place it back in the box. Cigarettes are expensive these days. While I have been diagnosed with stage one COPD, I don't want to quit. Smoking comforts me. It reminds me of my grandfather in Greece who smoked four packs of cigarettes a day. I get back into my SUV. Luckily, I am wearing a heavy parka. Despite the cold, I fall asleep.

Years ago, after I lost my job working as a sales clerk at Michael's, I was evicted from my house in Palmdale. I ended up living in my GMC Safari van for about a year. During the day, I drove around aimlessly. I was able to join the YMCA, so I could take a shower at least every other day. Since I drank like a fish, I blacked out a lot and somehow ended up in a Wal-Mart parking lot at night. That's a hot spot for the homeless. I received food stamps and General relief, but that wasn't enough to survive. My cigarettes were more expensive than other brands, and I smoked two packs a day back then. Even though my grandfather died of lung cancer at the age of eighty, I still smoked.

Even though I have not slept in a car for over a decade, I have perfected the art.

My phone's alarm goes off. It's a little past eight. While the sun glows like a peach against the sky, I don't find beauty in its presence. I call Bakersfield Behavioral Healthcare Hospital and the nurse that picks up the phone after ten rings, tells me that she is in group therapy. I sigh with relief. She will be happy to hear that I have rescued her dog. I owe her that much.

The shelter is quiet when I arrive promptly at 8:45 am. The German shepherd, husky and terrier are still there, but the other cages are empty. Didn't the officer say that the vet would not be here until nine? What happened? Where is Buddha?

I panic.

The animal control officer with the purple and white talons is replaced with a kindlier woman whose face belies the sadness of working at this place.

"Where is Buddha?" I ask.

"In the back with Dr. Green. Getting his shots and a microchip."

"Okay," I say.

"I am so happy you are adopting him! He is a good boy. He deserves better than an owner surrendering him to the pound."

I don't feel like telling her that it was entirely my fault that caused Buddha to end up at the Lake Isabella shelter. All I want to do is retrieve the dog, and get the hell out of there.

After I pay the adoption fee, Buddha emerges from the back, along with a young blonde-haired female vet tech. When Buddha sees me, he joyfully wags his tail. While I feel a sense of shame swoop over me, I am happy and full of hope.

As we drive away from the shelter, I check my rear view mirror. Buddha is curled up on the passenger seat, like one of those little squiggly bugs that crunch up when you touch them. The dog is exhausted from his ordeal. I have to call the psych ward before we hit the 178 West because there is no phone signal. How the hell did I ever end up in Kern County? I lived in Beverly Hills in Los Angeles after I left Chicago. Being here in the land of the living dead had never been on my agenda. While I have become quite prosperous during sobriety obtaining credit cards and a brand new white Lexus SUV, as a single woman, a house in Wofford Heights had been the more affordable option.

After fifteen rings, the nurse picks up. When I ask if I can talk to her, the nurse says, "She was released an hour ago."

"What?" I say, taken aback.

"We had to empty some beds. Her hold is up."

"It's because she has Medical, right? Your rooms are for patients with private insurance, right?"

"Please don't raise your voice at me," she says.

"How can you let her go? She's a mess!"

"The doctor determined that she was fit to leave," she says.

"How the hell is she going to get to Lake Isabella from Bakersfield?" I scream.

"There are buses," the nurse said. "And she has her phone with her."

"There's no goddamn signal in the canyon," I say.

"Please don't curse," says the nurse.

"Fuck you!" I scream.

The nurse hangs up.

I dial her number. The call goes right to voicemail. Right on my rear is an asshole in a brand new black Ford pick up truck. I pull over to a turn out to get out of his way. As he drives by, he gives me the finger.

"Asshole!" I scream.

When I reach to 178, I lose the cell phone signal. Damn it. I can't make a U-turn on the freeway. All I can do is drive through the canyon heading for Bakersfield, and then what? Where is she? How do I find her? She doesn't have any money to take the bus!

As if he senses something amiss, Buddha wakes up, and sits upright in the seat. He looks out the window.

I imagine her walking down the canyon that curves like a rattlesnake about to strike. Kern River is cruel and relentless and has taken many lives. Huge rocks surround the river, which is like a silver belt, an abusive father ready to belt his child. By car, Bakersfield is 56 miles away from Lake Isabella.

The sun disappears, and the sky turns cloudy. I turn on my headlights, and my car twists and turns through the canyon like a firefly.

Or a lightning bug, as she calls them. When she was a kid, she collected insects. For science class, she made a school project.

"My project was called, *What is the effect of Tabasco on wasps*?" she says. "Teacher said I was mean to the wasps. I got an F. I felt so guilty. Years later, I became a vegan."

We are working on her fifth step, and naturally, the science teacher is on her list of resentments on her fourth step inventory.

"God, I hated that teacher," she says. "Mrs. Stern. How apropos."

I peer at the inventory. While I told her to write it out, she did not listen. It is typed out.

"I see that you are on the top of the resentment list," I say. I was not surprised. Many alcoholics exhibit a lot of self-hatred.

As I drive up the 178, Buddha stares out the window, a worried look on his face. They always say dogs have a sixth sense. But I have a sixth sense too. Ever since I got sober, I feel like it's easier for me to get in touch with my intuition. That doesn't always happen. My intuition is as tiny as the pilot flame in an old gas panel. Sometimes it blows out. But when it's lit, I can sense things, both good and bad, before they happen.

Halfway through the canyon, I see the ambulance, along with two police cars. Luckily, I brake in time, because traffic has slowed down, and cars are bumper to bumper. The moron who gave me the finger is in front of me blasting country music, and beeping his horn. I drive closer to the scene, which is surrounded by yellow police tape. I see coroners lifting a body bag onto a stretcher. The police wave at me, telling me to keep driving.

Buddha frantically scratches the passenger door.

"I know her. I know her," I say, but the police tell me to keep moving.

Her cell phone indicates that the last number she called is the shelter. Turns out that the kindly woman who helped me informed her that Buddha had been adopted. But the woman did not tell her the identity of the person who adopted the dog, because for some stupid reason, that is against shelter policy. While I had saved Buddha's life, I could not save hers.

After I identify her body, I contact her relatives in Chicago who have not talked to her in years. I make sure that she is embalmed before her body is shipped back to Chicago. Besides paying for the embalmment, I pay for the flight. At the airport, I have to fill out so much paperwork. And then finally, while other passengers laugh and talk on their cell phones in the airport waiting area, I stand there with my face pressed against the glass window, watching a brown box being loaded into cargo. She is heading back home, for the first time in over a decade. After the last passenger boards the plane, I wait. What am I waiting for? When the plane takes off, I head back to my car. Buddha sits on the driver's seat, his face pressed against the window waiting for me to arrive.

We drive to Pet Smart so that I can get him a new nametag and a brand new leather collar. The tag is engraved with my phone number and includes his name, as well as my last name, along with the words, Buddha's Mommy. The tag is shiny blue, in the shape of a bone.

On the long drive home, I listen to Soundgarden.

"But you're staring at me, like I, like I need to be saved, saved like I need to be saved, saved..."

The Madwoman of Wigs

Bertha's mistress sobbed behind the closed pink door of her bedroom. Ceramic doll head planters holding rose and Venus fly trap bouquets atop Americana style tables were lined up along the corridor. Much to her dismay, Bertha saw Varicella, the Chihuahua strutting down the corridor like a KGB soldier. The dog wore a golden ballerina gown, and a diamond studded collar. The sobbing drowned out the first movement of Wagner's *Ride of the Valkyries*, which blared from the den. Mr. Simon De La Delaware opened the den's door. While he smoked a cigar, he guzzled a glass of scotch like a pelican swallowing fish. Even though he never went anywhere, he always wore a tuxedo.

"Another box arrived this morning," he said.

"What do you mean, sir?" asked Bertha.

"Wake up and smell the roses," he said.

He went back into the den, and slammed the door hard. One of the vases crashed onto the floor, spilling water all over the white rug. Bertha shivered, as she saw the doll's eyes staring blankly ahead, covered by shards. The Wagner caused the walls to shake. Behind the bedroom door, the mistress's sobbing turned into wailing that sounded like a chorus in a Greek tragedy.

Bertha knocked on the door.

"Death will become me!" Mrs. De La Delaware screamed.

"Madame, please, I beg you, let me in!"

Varicella hovered around Bertha's feet, yipping.

The door opened slightly. Before she could find refuge, the dog bit Bertha's ankle. Like a war hero, Mrs. De La Delaware pulled Bertha to safety and slammed the door on Varicella's face.

The pink room contained Mrs. D.'s private touch, because after all, Mr. D. slept in the den. Sphinx, Mrs. D's standard white poodle sat on top of the king sized bed. The dog wore a ruby studded collar, along with a platinum blonde wig. Besides the wig on Sphinx's head, the room contained different shades of blonde, brown and black wigs. There must have been about 200 or so wigs crammed in every nook and cranny of the room. Scattered on the bed, running amuck on the floor, and perched on mannequins' heads, the wigs dominated the room. Even the replica statue of the Venus De Milo had a black Veronica Lake style wig perched on its head. In the corner of the room, next to a bar, was the large order that had arrived to the residence that morning. Shivering, Bertha wondered how many wigs were in that unopened box.

Hanging from the walls, were framed pictures featuring Mrs. D's commercial wig ads. One print depicted a younger Mrs. D. in a white chiffon dress, smoking a cigarette. A black Bettie Page wig rested on her head. The caption, which was superimposed on the upper half of the print, read, BETTE BANG BANGS. Another ad featured Mrs. D. in a sexy black dress. Her vintage blonde up do was crammed with golden bobby pins. The caption read, DO YOU DIG THE WIG? DO THE PINS MAKE YOU SPIN?

"Darling, can you make me a martini?" said Mrs. D, smiling. Since Bertha had walked into the room, Mrs. D. had calmed down considerably. From a snarling tyrannosaurus rex, she had transformed into a serene sea urchin. Her outfit, however, was far from calm. Mrs. D. wore a pink poodle skirt, along with a black sleeveless shirt and penny loafers. Besides the poodle, a flamingo was camouflaged on the skirt. As Mrs. D. adjusted her wig cap, she beckoned with her cigarette holder.

"Skip the olives, make it a Gibson," Mrs. D. said, as she took a long drag from her cigarette.

"Madam, did you take your sleeping pills. It might not be wise to drink," said Bertha.

Yes, drink! Bottoms up, you old crone!

"Thank you for caring so much about me, sweetheart," said Mrs. D. "I'm sure I will be fine."

Outside a large glass window was the skyline. Buildings glowed like lightning bugs. In the distance, Bertha saw the tip of the Empire State building, which she admired when she first came to the Big Apple from North Dakota. Now she had other thoughts.

I want to climb up that damn building like King Kong and jump. I can't take it anymore. I have completely lost my mind in this house of horrors. And what's with the goddamn poodle skirt? She's pushing seventy!

"I'm thirsty, darling," Mrs. D. said.

Once upon a time, Bertha thought. *I was a young chorus girl, dancing and singing in Broadway shows like "Kiss Me Kate," and "Oklahoma!" But then mama became ill, and I had to go back to Buttzville. When mama died, I came back. No one wanted me, not even my agent who once said that I would be a shining star on Broadway. Look at me now. Sweet lord, heavenly father, look at me now.*

"Hey, Tolstoy. Are you writing *War and Peace*?" said Mrs. D., chuckling.

"No, Madame," said Bertha, as she garnished the drink with small onions. Oh how she wanted to substitute poison for the vermouth! Oh, how she wanted to flee from Central Park West and buy a one-way ticket to Siberia so that she could go into exile! The idea of freezing to death and losing her toes to frostbite was more appealing than this present day nightmare! But perhaps Siberia was too far fetched. Bellevue was within walking distance. Bellevue would be her Mecca. Even solitary confinement sounded wonderful compared to living in the San Remo at the mercy of Mrs. De La Delaware.

For the next hour or so, Mrs. D. guzzled Gibson after Gibson, smoking cigarette after cigarette. She tried on one wig after another, asking, over and over, "Bertha, which one looks best with my complexion?"

This was a little game that Mrs. D. played with Bertha. The trick was to smile like an idiot and remain silent until Mrs. D. had tried on all of her wigs. After Mrs. D. took the last wig off her ugly head, and asked, for the final time, "Bertha, which one looks best with my complexion?"

The correct answer that would save Bertha's hide was, "Madame, all of the wigs look best with your complexion."

When they first played the game, and Mrs. D. asked Bertha, "Bertha, which one looks best with my complexion?" Bertha said, with utmost honesty. "Madame, the strawberry blonde wig looks really pretty on you. It lights up your face."

Mrs. D.'s reaction took her by surprise. The old crone screamed. She opened her closet door, and one by one, hurled shoes at Bertha. Like the wigs, there were over 200 pairs of shoes, including roller skates and Eskimo boots in that damn closet! After a penny loafer struck her on the head, Bertha fell on the ground, as if she were a soldier wounded in the trenches, during the battle at Gettysburg. While Mrs. D. hurled shoes at her, the damn Sphinx sneered.

After the shoe attack ended, Bertha limped off to her room, and cried. How she wanted to leave! But where could she go? Her despicable brother had inherited mama's house. He sold it and gambled the money away! Then, he made some people angry, ran down to Tijuana where he got kicked in the head by a donkey! Now he was dead!

If only I could be so lucky, thought Bertha.

That night, after the first wig game, Bertha had a nightmare that she was running through Central Park, being chased by Cruella De Ville who was driving a pink Jaguar XK120. The next day, while Mrs. D. took her afternoon nap, Bertha confided in Maude, the cook.

"You must tell her that all of the wigs look best with her complexion," sighed Maude, as she prepared prime rib for Varicella. Like Mrs. D., who loved animals, Sphinx was a vegetarian and ate special meals prepared by Maude, of course.

"*Best?* Is that even grammatically correct?" asked Bertha.

"Please heed my words. Or misfortune awaits."

"What do you mean?"

"The last maid who did not play the game stole Mrs. D.'s sleeping pills and well." Maude sighed. "Our beloved Varicella found her on your bed. Had vomit all over the mattress. Poor thing. She had no family. Ended up in a pauper's grave."

Bertha stared.

"Don't worry. I scrubbed the mattress with bleach," said Maude.

From that point on, Bertha slept on the floor of her tiny room that had once been a walk-in closet. She also heeded Maude's advice. When they played the stupid wig game, and Mrs. D. asked, "Bertha, which one looks best with my complexion?" Bertha responded in a mechanical voice, as if she were Robert the Robot that is, that is if that hunk of plastic could speak, "Madame, all of the wigs look best with your complexion."

One day, Bertha had a migraine.

Perhaps its from sleeping on that damn floor, she thought.

When Mrs. D. beckoned her, Bertha trudged up the stairs. Even Varicella gave her a look of pity, and stood aside letting her pass. Finally, she approached Mrs. D.s' boudoir. Since the door was open, she let herself in.

"My, my, my," said Mrs. D. "You are a little tardy."

"My head hurts," said Bertha.

"Come, come! Many wigs to explore!"

As Bertha stifled a yawn, Mrs. D. tried on a few wigs, including a platinum blonde bouffant, and finally, a white wig that had a small ponytail.

Oh, my God. That's a Louis the XV wig, Bertha thought.

"Bertha, which one looks best with my complexion?" asked Mrs. D, as she applied white powder onto the stupid white wig.

Bertha remained silent.

"Wait till you see my Marie Antoinette wig," said Mrs. D. pointing to Sphinx, who was wearing the three foot high monstrosity.

Even though I am almost 35, I still have some time left. But I don't care anymore! What have I done to deserve this madwoman of wigs? What?

As Mrs. D. tried on the Marie Antoinette wig, Bertha cast a look of despair at Sphinx. The dog sneered.

"Bertha, which one looks best with my complexion?"

OOOOk-lahoma, where the wind comes sweepin' down the plain, And the wavin' wheat can sure smell sweet, When the wind comes right behind the rain.

This time, Mrs. D. asked, with menace in her voice.

"Bertha, which one looks best with my complexion?"

Bertha snickered.

As the wig lady hurled shoes at her, Bertha became hysterical with laughter. Sphinx barked. Suddenly, she felt something hard hit her on the head, followed by another hard object, but her hysteria grew in volume. Somehow the damn wig fell of Mrs. D's wig, and ended up into the dog's mouth.Before she blacked out, she saw the roller skates that Mrs. D. had used as a weapon.

When Bertha woke up, her head ached.

She was at Bellevue Hospital.

"You have a mild concussion, young lady," said the kindly, aging doctor. "I am sorry you hit your head on a tub. Just a little aspirin and rest for the next few days, and you'll be good as new." As he spoke, his dentures rattled like maracas.

"What tub? I was attacked by a wig whacko," she said.

"A sense of humor is delightful," the doctor said.

"On my mother's grave, I swear to you, I have lost my mind," she said. "Please move me to the psych ward."

"You seem perfectly sane to me, young lady," said the doctor.

"I'm not young, you stupid fool!" she yelled.

"I'm sorry you're upset," he said, with a sigh. "Well, you might feel better when you go home. The De La Delawares are on their way." As he spoke, she gaped at the black wig that sat on top of his head. Strands of black hair crawled onto his forehead like a tarantula's legs. Before he had the chance to realize what was happening, Bertha yanked the tarantula wig off his head. She jumped up, and kicked the old doctor in the groin. As he howled in pain, she ran out of the room, along with the wig, in a hospital gown and bare feet. After she positioned the wig on her head, she sprinted down the corridor. She almost ran into a nurse pushing an elderly man in a wheelchair down the passageway. Then she continued running down the hall, with the tarantula wig bopping up and down her head, singing, "*We know we belong to the land, And the land we belong to is grand! And when we say, Yeeow! A-yip-i-o-e-ay! We're only sayin', You're doin' fine, Oklahoma! Oklahoma, O.K.*"

When the De La Delaware's arrived, the doctor told them that Bertha was in the psychiatric ward, and would be there for an indefinite period of time. Perhaps they should hire another maid.

The Locket

For a Saturday afternoon, Isaiah's Nook Thrift Store in Southlake was empty. Behind the glass counter, near the vintage cash register, there was a white haired female store clerk who scrutinized antique porcelain dolls that were propped on shelves against the wall. The old lady wore a gray cotton housedress that was probably sewn during the Great Depression. A vintage Tiffany chandelier with three pull chain light switches hung over the counter, casting an ambient glow. When Molly saw the white porcelain locket, which radiated like a pearl against soft light, she smiled softly. While the ornament was nestled against an array of gaudy costume jewelry, the locket glowed proudly. There was a clasp on the locket, which was set in gold metal. Molly wondered if the locket contained a cameo.

"Can I see this locket?" Molly asked, staring at the old woman, who did not respond. Clutching her feather duster, the woman swayed like a shaman performing a trance dance. The dolls stared ahead, a captive audience. The old lady spoke, without turning around.

"Estate donation."

"What?"

"Locket."

"Can I look at it?"

The old lady turned around. She stared at Molly with glazed blue eyes. Her face had wrinkles deeper than the grooves on a fungal toenail. The old woman had an old-fashioned transistor hearing aid propped on one ear like a boomerang. Her plastic nametag, which glowed against her dress, identified her as Lamia.

"Interesting name. Lamia," said Molly. "Is it Greek?"

"Good golly, Miss Molly! That ain't none of your goddamn beeswax!" said Lamia.

Molly's eyes opened wide.

How the hell did this lunatic know her name?

Next to the dolls, an old fashioned cuckoo clock's pendulum struck the hour. An automated bird emerged, moving with each note. It was 5 pm.

As if she read Molly's mind, Lamia said, "Small town. Ain't take long around these parts to know who's who. You ain't from around here, I reckon."

"No," sighed Molly. "I'm from LA."

"You sure is far away from Angel City," Lamia laughed. Then, she said, "Anyhow, lady's family donated books. Some classics, others dime store paperbacks. But if ya' fixin' to find a treasure I'd head over yonder right now."

She pointed towards the back of the store.

How did this woman know she was looking for books?

"You look like one of them hoity toity writers I read about," said Lamia, as if she read Molly's thoughts.

"Virginia Woolf?"

"Yeah, the one with the big schnozz who drown herself," asked Lamia, chuckling. "Probably stunk like kyarn when they dug up the corpse."

"Kyarn?"

"Road kill," said Lamia with a grin.

"I'd really like to look at the locket, if you don't mind," said Molly.

"You got champagne tastes and a beer budget, huh, girlie?" said the woman.

Molly's cheeks burned with shame.

"Locket ain't got feet. First, I'd go check out those books you fixin' to get. Some in boxes. Others in tow sacks. Tick tock tick tock. Go on, now."

Suddenly, Lamia glared at her, with a look of hatred. The Tiffany lamp's bulb flickered, casting a dim light on her wrinkled face, making her pupils the color of topaz. Molly felt a chill, as if she were inside a morgue. Out of the corner of her eyes, she noticed a porcelain doll dressed in red velvet apparel gazing at her. Closing her eyes, Molly took a few deep breaths. When she opened her eyes, the doll stared straight ahead. Lamia's back was turned to her, and she was dusting the dolls. Molly shook her head. While she suffered from bipolar disorder, her psychiatrist had prescribed Latuda, which was an anti-psychotic. Sometimes she saw and heard things that were not real. The Latuda was supposed to get rid of those symptoms. Maybe she needed a higher dose.

She heard a sound behind her, and jumped.

"Sorry about that. Need to change the bulb."

Molly turned to see a kindly bald headed man in his fifties walking towards her. He wore a *Disciple* rock band t-shirt, jeans and dirty sneakers. His plastic nametag identified him as Isaiah.

"Looking for anything in particular?" he asked.

"I collect old books."

"Come with me."

She followed him to the back of the store where there were boxes and burlap sacks crammed with books. Molly sighed. How could she sort through all these boxes?

Isaiah smiled.

"Give me a few days. I'll put aside some old books for you. Before you leave, I'll write down the store's phone number. But wait a sec."

He walked over to a shelf and tugged out a large Bible. As he handed the book to her, she cringed as if he had given her a hot plate. She quickly composed herself, but his eyes had not missed a thing.

"You Christian?" he asked.

"Born and raised Catholic," she said, as she studied the Bible. The hardcover book had a blue velvet cover, with golden letters. She flipped through the pages, and studied the title page. Her eyes opened when she saw that the Bible had been printed in 1905.

"Douay–Rheims version," Isaiah said.

"I know," she said.

"You go to Church?"

"Not anymore. I converted to atheism."

"And the Pharisees and the scribes grumbled, saying, "This man receives sinners and eats with them," said Isaiah. "Luke 15:2."

"I am familiar with the New Testament," said Molly.

Who the hell did this guy wearing a stupid Disciple t-shirt think he was?

"I went to a Catholic High School. I saw enough nuns there to last ten lifetimes," she said.

"Christians do not believe in reincarnation," he said.

Oh, shut up.

If Isaiah gave her a good price, she would purchase the Bible, sell it on E-bay and make a nice profit. The Bible was an antique, and probably worth a lot of money. Hopefully, this guy would cut her a deal. He didn't seem like an idiot but he did appear concerned that she was a nonbeliever. Maybe he would sell the Bible to her for cheap, in the hopes that he could save her doomed soul.

Clutching the Bible, Molly followed Isaiah to the front of the store. Lamia was gone. Before Molly asked Isaiah about the crazy old woman, she noticed that the locket necklace was hanging around the neck of the creepy porcelain doll. Did Lamia drape the necklace around the doll?

"Can I see that locket?"

"What locket?"

Molly pointed at the doll. As Isaiah handed the locket to Molly, he shook his head, a perplexed look on his face. "Didn't catch my eyes till now. That doll came in yesterday, with other items from a woman's estate. Probably belonged to the dead woman."

Molly caught a glimpse of her reflection in an oval mirror propped on the counter. Besides the deep-set wrinkles that formed a gothic-style arch over her mouth, the bags under her eyes were as puffy as blowfishes. Suddenly, depression permeated her soul like rotten food rising out of a clogged sink.

After Molly put the locket around her neck, she cast another look in the mirror. The locket cast a beautiful glow against her skin, giving the illusion that her face was smooth and young. Her depression was replaced by jubilation. Suddenly, Molly wanted to grab Isaiah, and plant a huge kiss on his bland face.

"It suits your complexion," said Isaiah.

"How much is it?" she asked, as she handed the locket back to him.

As Isaiah examined the ornament, he tried to open the clasp, which did not budge. After a moment, he sighed.

"Jesus said it is better to give than to receive," said Molly.

Isaiah chuckled.

"Twenty, no tax for the Bible," he said. "I have to charge tax for the locket otherwise my accountant will have a heyday. How's $25.00 plus tax?"

Molly gasped with joy.

"Can I pay cash for the Bible, and put the locket on my credit card?"

"Works for me," said Isaiah.

While Isaiah separately rang up the items, Molly happily placed the locket inside her bag. Then she noticed a solemn expression on his face. He said, "The woman died by hanging. I should have told you sooner."

"Maybe its haunted," laughed Molly. "That would be interesting."

Isaiah cast her a horrified look. Then, he took a deep breath and said, "I have something else for you."

He crouched down, and searched throughout stacks of books, which were on the floor, behind the counter.

Great, thought Molly. How long is this going to take? But he was nice to me, so I better behave. Suddenly, she heard a chuckle, and looked up. Did the doll just laugh? And why did the doll sound like Lamia?

After what seemed like an eternity, Isaiah handed her a paperback Bible along with the receipts for the purchases. "New American Standard. This is a gift."

"Thanks," she muttered, as she shoved the receipts inside the paperback.

"'Jesus said to him, "Away from me, Satan! For it is written: 'Worship the Lord your God, and serve him only,'" he said.

"What?" she asked.

"Matthew 4:10," he said. "These words will protect you from evil."

Was this a thrift store or a little shop of horrors?

An hour later, she walked into her small one bedroom house where she lived alone, in Lake Isabella. She placed the Bibles and the locket on a table. As she lit a cigarette, she surveyed her house. Dishes were stacked up in the sink. Bills were still in sealed envelopes. Empty coffee mugs and dirty clothing were scattered all over a filthy rug that desperately needed vacuuming, followed by a heavy-duty shampoo. The only spotless area in the house was a bookshelf, which displayed her antique books. Molly shivered. While her gas had been cut off, because she could not afford to pay the bill last month, she had a fireplace. When the wood burned, the aroma comforted her. Maybe that's why she collected books, too. Books soothed Molly, reminding her of the grandmother who read to her when she was a little girl. Before her grandmother died, she gave Molly a first edition of Virginia Woolf's *The Waves*. She knew Molly wanted to be a writer. Even though her parents laughed at that idea, her grandmother did not. These days Molly lived off her disability because one day, a few years prior, she tried to kill herself, and ended up in a psychiatric ward. Even though she still suffered from bipolar disorder, she hoped that one day she would pursue her dream. Remembering the Latuda, she called her psychiatrist.

After she left a message in his voicemail, she lit a fire in the fireplace. Then she gazed at the locket that beckoned her, like a toddler gesturing to be picked up.

Inside the bathroom, she placed the locket around her neck. She caught a glimpse of her reflection in the mirror. She was stunning! Why was it that she had never noticed this before?

As she fingered the locket, the spring clasp released to reveal a cameo made from a daguerreotype of a beautiful woman wearing a Puritan bonnet. While sharp, the silvery image appeared eerie and ghostlike. Back in college, one of her favorite classes was history of photography. She remembered that the daguerreotype process used silver-plated copper plates that were approximately six by eight inches. How could this cameo have been made? Obviously, the locket was valuable.

After she took her medication, she flipped through the Bible that Isaiah had given her until she found the receipts. When she looked at the locket's invoice, she frowned. How could this be? She paid $25.00 for the locket, with a total sales price of $34.14? Wouldn't an eight percent sales tax result in a final price that was lower than $34.14? Then she saw that Isaiah had scrawled his first name with black magic marker under the thrift store's address and phone number.

Slowly, she placed the Bible back on the table.

After she poked the embers around in the fireplace, she changed into a t-shirt and leggings. The fire would die out in a few hours or so. Then, she took her medication, ate a glazed donut, smoked another cigarette and grabbed a bottle of water from the refrigerator. Every night, Molly performed her bedtime rituals like clockwork. After she brushed her teeth, she went to sleep, with the locket pressed against her heart.

Like a metronome, the sound of knocking against her door occurred in regular intervals, with absolute precision.

Startled, Molly woke up and looked at her alarm clock.

It was 3 am.

Molly stumbled into the dining room, turned on the light, and the knocking stopped. Then she ran to the door, and locked the deadbolts. After that, she checked the windows, making sure that they were shut. She caught a glimpse of her reflection inside the hallway mirror. She was no longer beautiful. Her wrinkles looked like furrows plowed in the ground for planting seeds. Suddenly, the locket sprang open to reveal another cameo.

Molly peered closer to see.

The image was a post-mortem daguerreotype of her! She was dead, with her eyes clamped shut!

Then the locket slammed shut.

Molly's heart pounded. She yanked at the necklace but it would not budge. She tried to open the locket, but it was shut tight like a coffin.

This is not a psychotic episode, she thought. This is really happening.

Trembling, she poured herself a glass of wine, and lit a cigarette. Then she collapsed on a chair, staring at the two Bibles.

There was another knock, and another, and another.

Then there was silence.

She ran to the window, where she peeked out behind the curtains. Outside, streetlamps lit the empty street. The porch light cast a glow on the walkway. An elderly woman, wearing an early 20th century style black dress with a bonnet marched away from her house. As if she scented Molly, the woman swung around, and strode back. As the woman approached closer to the window, Molly froze. Even though the bonnet covered most of her face, the woman's eyelids were shut, and her lips were blue. For a second, the woman disappeared. And then she was at Molly's door.

Molly loosened her grip on the windowsill, and backed into the dining room table. The receipt with Isaiah's phone number glided onto the floor.

Isaiah 34:14.

She flipped through the pages of the Catholic Bible.

While the creature's knocking grew louder, the doorknob rotated clockwise. It hesitated for a split second, and then the doorknob spun counter clockwise.

Molly tried to breathe, as the doorknob began to rattle.

Focus, she thought. Just focus.

"Isaiah 34:14. And demons and monsters shall meet, and the hairy ones shall cry out one to another, there hath the lamia lain down, and found rest for her self," Molly read loudly.

The Lamia?

Confused, Molly grabbed the New American Standard Version.

There was silence behind the door.

While the doorknob stopped moving, there was a tentative knock, followed by another, and another behind the door.

Desperately, Molly located Isaiah 34:14. While the meaning was the same, the words were different.

"The desert creatures will meet with the wolves, the hairy goat also will cry to its kind; Yes, the night monster will settle there. And will find herself a resting place," Molly read.

A resting place.

The knocking was getting louder and louder. Then Molly had a sudden realization.

Matthew 4:10.

Quickly, she flipped through the Book of Matthew until she found the verse, which popped out. It had been highlighted. She felt as if she was going to pass out, but she took a deep breathe and read, "Then Jesus said to him, "Go, Satan! For it is written, 'YOU SHALL WORSHIP THE LORD YOUR GOD, AND SERVE HIM ONLY!'"

Sudden silence. Molly tugged at the locket, and the necklace broke off. She hurled the locket necklace onto the dying embers in the fireplace. Flames rose up, as if she had thrown a match onto gasoline. Outside the door, she heard screaming, followed by the sound of footsteps running away, until there was silence. Suddenly, the flames collapsed, leaving smoldering remains.

Molly slowly got up from the floor and stumbled over to the window. Outside, on the porch a few feet away from her door, there was an old-fashioned transistor hearing aid, the size of a boomerang.

Odin

Agatha was in her late forties, and had been sober for over five years. She had long brown hair that needed trimming, and her penetrating brown eyes displayed an expression of disgust, as well as distrust.

She was skinny and glum, much like a thin wire inside a burnt light bulb. Once upon a time, she was full of light, and now she felt burned out. She smoked too many cigarettes, and drank too much coffee.

She had a sealed box of nicotine patches stacked on top of her Big Book, which she also used as a coaster for her coffee mug. The idea of putting a patch on her arm gave her the willies. Patches reminded her of leeches that doctors used on people during the 19th century. And she barely read her Big Book. That made her fall asleep.

Her sponsor told her to go to AA meetings, but she hardly did.

She hated AA meetings.

When she was sitting in a room full of recovering alcoholics, she felt like the filament inside a light bulb, as if she was cut off from the rest of the world by a film of white glass.

She did not like being around other women.

They put make up on while they admired themselves in mirrors.

It was hard for her to look at her own reflection. All she saw were sunken cheeks and a set of deep-set wrinkles that looked like ice tongs on each side of her mouth.

She promised herself that as soon as she had the money, she would get Botox and collagen injections. She wanted her face to be as smooth as the Gerber baby's, even though she was pushing fifty.

Because of the fact that she could not look at her reflection in the mirror, she did not like being around men, either. Most men in AA, well the ones she felt attracted to, over looked her, as if she was an outdated carton of eggs in the supermarket. Even though she was marked for clearance at a reduced price, the men chose to pay for the younger, fresher eggs.

And besides the fact that she was an old carton of eggs, there was another dilemma, when it came to men.

The dilemma came in the form of an eighty-pound blue nosed pit bull named Odin.

Four of her five dogs had been rescued from the pound. Odin had been rescued before he was sent to the pound. By a twist of fate, Agatha and Odin had been brought together.

Agatha had only three months of sobriety, the day she rescued the pit bull. She had been at an AA meeting in Palmdale. The meeting hall was in a small shopping mall, which included a pet food store.

After the meeting, most people socialized and smoked in front of the hall. She rapidly left, without saying goodbye, and headed over to the pet store to buy dog food. When she walked inside, she saw a rotund, blue nosed pit bull with a large head, lying inside a gold-colored pen in the center of the store. He reminded her of a baby hippopotamus that she once saw, so many moons ago, inside a large cage at the Bronx Zoo during an elementary school trip. His name was Odin. The barred enclosure to the hippo exhibit had large waterfall rocks, a pool, and lush greenery, to create the illusion of a wildlife setting. The hippo had a home, but he did not look too happy. According to the zoo guide, Odin's mother had recently been euthanized, after she had gotten very sick from a virus.

Agatha leaned against the black picket fence and peered. She could not see the young hippo. He was submerged in the pool. She stared at the young hippo, because she did not want to see what the other kids were doing. They were having too much fun, and she felt old and tired, even though she was only ten years old.

Most of the kids had family members with them. One mother took photos of her daughter. Another mother bought hot dogs and sodas for her son, and his friends. One girl strutted like a peacock, proudly displaying the large stuffed flamingo that her grandmother bought her from the gift store.

Agatha had an awful cream cheese sandwich from home inside her lunch box. The sandwich consisted of Wonder Bread and cream cheese. That was all she carried with her that day. Her mother had told her that there was no money to buy jelly, let alone a souvenir.

Odin was submerged in a pool, and his eyes were closed. He trembled. When he opened his eyes, Agatha thought his eyes looked watery, but perhaps it was just liquid from the pool. She believed that Odin was full of sorrow, because his mom had died.

I wish my mother would die, she thought.

As the class walked away from the exhibit, she threw her lunch bag into a waste can. Her stomach rumbled from hunger, but she didn't care.

Agatha heard the dog's stomach growling even though she was several feet away from him.

"He ran in here earlier, off the streets," said the storeowner. "No collar, nothing. Animal control is on their way to get him. They will probably euthanize but I can't bring him home. I have ten cats."

"I'll take him," she said.

The storeowner was taken aback.

"Are you sure?"

"Yes, I'll take him."

"Okay," said the storeowner. "Let me get someone to help you."

"Thank you," said Agatha.

The storeowner rang a bell, and a large, rugged male clerk materialized like the Good Witch of the North from the *Wizard of Oz*. He picked the dog up, threw him over his shoulders as if he was carrying a burlap bag full of rice, and followed Agatha, who was already outside, standing by her old white Toyota Corolla, smoking a cigarette. She paced back and forth like an expectant father. After she opened up the back door, the dog crawled across the leather seat, like a wounded soldier on a battlefield. He collapsed, and let out a sigh. He closed his eyes and fell asleep. As she petted his head, he placed his paw on top of her arm.

"You will be with me always," she said, like a little kid.

He responded with a snore.

On the way home, she thought of doggy names.

She settled on the name, Odin, in honor of the poor baby hippo. She also thought that the name of the Norwegian god might boost the poor dog's self-esteem. Agatha believed in the power of names, and hated her own name, which was Greek and translated to "naive." And God only knew, she had been green in many aspects of her life, a fact that she was not proud of.

She ran with Odin, and then walked the other four dogs, in teams of two. She bought them expensive dry dog food, and sometimes she cooked rice and chicken and fresh veggies inside a crockpot, and mixed the stew in with the dry food. Some guys in AA thought she was nuts, and that she harbored a canine addiction. But the real issue, which made dating a worthless venture to pursue, was Odin.

From the scared dog that she first met, Odin became an overly protective companion that guarded her like one of the soldiers at Buckingham Palace. Any time she tried to bring a man over to her house, there was Odin, with his floppy ears, and large square head, staring out the window like the pig from *The Amityville Horror* movie. He looked like a Jack O' Lantern with his two glowing eyes. After the date caught a glimpse of Odin's eyes smoldering through the dark window, the guy never called again.

She gave up dating, which was a good thing. It was too much work balancing a relationship and a pack of dogs, and honestly she preferred her dogs over a stupid guy.

Since she had too many dogs, she ran into issues at the houses that she lived in. She either got evicted for one of two reasons. The first being, she had lied on the housing application about the number of dogs that she had, and even worse, had not told the landlord that she had pit bulls. For some reason, landlords hated pit bulls, and that always pissed her off, so why should she be honest on the application? The second reason was because she was prone to really bad depression, and sometimes she could not get out of bed. When she got depressed, she huddled under the covers with her dogs instead of showing up at work.

Inevitably, she would lose her job, get served with an eviction notice due to nonpayment of rent, and ended up at court. Somehow, she lucked out by getting a sympathetic judge or court mediator, who granted her an extended stay at her residence, without her having to pay any money to the landlord. During the interim, she always landed another job. While she had a degree in photography, and usually worked as a photographer's assistant, she was a self-taught waitress and bartender. Besides taking pictures, she was great at slinging hash, serving cups of Joe and mixing outdated Woo Woo's. Between the new job and getting free rent, she was able to save money, and acquire another home for her and the pooches.

Because she was desperate, she ended up in awful houses, that weren't fit to house a canine, let alone a human. These dumps were usually located in the outskirts of rural areas that no single female in her right mind would ever live in. But she felt safe, because of the dogs.

Agatha's latest dismal hovel was a mobile home in the Mojave Desert. The only nice thing about this scrappy structure was that the landlord had approved all of her dogs, and had even met Odin, who oddly enough had not growled at him. Aside from that, the house was nestled on two acres littered with old cars, baby diapers, a broken Jacuzzi, plastic bags, and waste. Joshua trees were strewn everywhere, and at night, when she looked out the window, there was a tree that looked like the grim reaper.

During the day, the sun harshly beat against her windows, and she developed migraines. At night, the wind blew through holes in the floors, and cracks through the windows. The Mojave had the worst wind, and often Agatha felt that the house would be ripped off by a cyclone, and like Dorothy and Toto, she would end up in Oz with Odin, Freya, Layla, Loki and Zelda.

But there were worse issues.

The landlord told Agatha that she had to share an electric meter with a weird couple, who lived a few feet away, in a garage converted into a makeshift house. The oval faced girl was about twenty-five, long dark hair, sunken eyes and no eyebrows. Her bald boyfriend, who delivered oxygen for a living, shot words out of his mouth, like an Uzi spraying bullets. The guy was about twenty years older than the pothead girlfriend, who was also addicted to meth. At night, Agatha heard them screaming and glass smashing, while their three dogs, Precious, Bella and Baby barked.

During the day, they left Bella, an underweight shepherd mix outside. The dog was locked in a kennel that was way too small for her. To top it off, the neighbors did not leave her with any food or water. Her hungry cries wore Agatha out. Agatha wanted to call animal control on her neighbors, but she was afraid of retaliation.

Sharing the meter was a nightmare. There was no heat in the house, and Agatha relied on electric heaters to keep her and the dogs warm. The neighbors blasted their air conditioner non-stop during the summer, and turned their electric heaters up to the highest voltage during the winter. The worst part was that the electric bill was in Agatha's name. After she moved in, the landlord showed up at her house, screaming and told her that she had to transfer the bill in her name. When she told the landlord to approach the neighbor, who had moved in before her, he said that he had knocked on the neighbor's door, called about fifty times, left a message on his voicemail and had not heard back. Then he told Agatha that he was going to shut off the electricity that day if neither of them placed the bill in their name.

Instead of standing up to herself, she called the electric company and dutifully complied with the landlord's demands. Initially, the neighbors paid half of the bill, according to the terms of the lease. Suddenly, they stopped giving Agatha any money. It had been three months since she had seen a dime from them. And what did Agatha do?

Being a woman who was afraid of conflict, she made courteous phone calls, and sent polite texts to the neighbors. The bald guy kept promising her that he would pay his share as soon as he got his paycheck. He never did.

And Agatha, whose most recent job was working as a photographer at a wedding studio in the Valley, kept making payments on the electric bill, because it was in her name. One customer service rep at the electric company said, "That was a bad idea. Putting the bill in your name. You are responsible for the entire amount."

She asked the landlord to intervene, and he refused. He said he was undergoing kidney dialysis, and he had other issues to worry about.

As a result of this nightmare, her rent became late.

Agatha called the landlord and tried to reason with him. She asked if he could wait a few weeks for the rent. Reluctantly, he agreed. Afterwards she went to the neighbor's house, knocked on the door and demanded the money that was owed to her. The bald guy came running out, and screamed. He threatened to call the pound on her, even though her dogs had done nothing, and he was abusive to poor Bella. Then, he slammed the door in her face, making Agatha fall backwards. She stumbled on an empty oxygen tank that was outside his door and fell to the ground. After she got up, bruised and dirty, she knocked on his door again, and heard him scream, "Fuck you!" Frightened, she ran back to her own house, and cried.

Like she did, long ago, when her mom used to make those awful cream cheese sandwiches, she lost her appetite. She became skinnier than she already was, and her cheeks grew more sunken. Who the hell would want her taking photos at a wedding? She looked like a corpse!

A few days after the argument with the neighbor, she heard the alarm clock go off. It was only 6 am, and she had a wedding ceremony to shoot at noon in the San Fernando Valley. She turned the alarm off, and crawled back under the covers. Her dogs were on the bed. Odin nestled against her, put his head on her arm, and went back to sleep. She closed her eyes, and had a horrible nightmare that her crazed neighbor was pursuing her, in his oxygen delivery van. When she woke up, it was five pm.

Instead of firing her, her boss, Tony told her that she could not shoot weddings anymore. He gave her another position. Instead of taking photos with her Nikon at lavish marriage ceremonies followed by expensive receptions, she edited wedding and engagement photos, in Photoshop on a Mac computer at the studio.

For eight hours a day, she edited image after image. Most were variations of the same theme. There was the happy bride smiling, or baring her teeth like a mule. There was the groom grinning like an idiotic schoolboy, and making ludicrous hand gestures like a rap artist. Carefully, Agatha removed blemishes, and wrinkles, often wishing she could Photoshop her own facial wrinkles. Besides removing imperfections off their stupid faces, she added highlights to their complexions. Noses were adjusted. Chins were shortened. Strands of fly about hair were removed. Agatha created vignettes, giving the illusion that the happy bride and groom were surrounded by a white halo. She made black and white photos, leaving the pinks and reds in the wedding bouquets. Another one of her duties was creating slide shows for engagement parties, and wedding receptions. The happy bride and groom gave her loads of old baby photos, and all of those photos had to be scanned and inserted into the slide show. And then there was the soundtrack. That was the worst part. The sentimental wedding music made her skin crawl.

One happy couple gave her a song that made her fall over in her seat.

"Imagine me and you, I do, I think about you day and night, it's only right, to think about the girl you love and hold her tight, so happy together."

"I can't see me lovin' nobody but you for all my life," Agatha hummed, under her breath, as she drove home from a long day at the studio. "When you're with me, baby, the skies will be blue for all my life."

She was exhausted from working on that engagement slide show, trying to synchronize the sappy Turtles song with an assortment of bride and groom photos. When she drove up to the house, she saw Odin peering through the window. Then, she saw the faces of her other dogs pop up, like marionette puppets, and her face lit up. She continued singing. "Me and you, and you and me. No matter how they tossed the dice, it had to be." And then she looked up and saw a three-day notice to pay or quit taped on the front door. For hours or so it seemed she stared at the notice, which had been ruthlessly attached on her door, with duct tape, while her dogs yelped from inside the house.

Once again, she texted the neighbor, asking for his share of the electric bill, but this time, he told the landlord that she was harassing him. The landlord called. He insisted that she stop communicating with the neighbor, or else he would file a police report. When she asked about the money the neighbor owed her, the landlord said, "You lied to me!"

"About what? My dogs? You knew how many dogs I had," she said.

"I did some research on you! You told me you have never been evicted," he said. "That's a lie!"

Then, he hung up.

Frantically, she called a legal service that helped tenants with low incomes in the hopes that she could get help with the eviction. Even though she was more than familiar with the eviction process, she became overwhelmed and terrified. The paralegal told her to call back when she was served with unlawful detainer papers.

"The unlawful detainer is part of the eviction process," the paralegal said.

"I know," Agatha said, feeling ashamed. "I have been through this before."

"Okay, well then, call us when you get served," said the paralegal.

"What about the neighbor who isn't paying his share of the bill? That's what started this mess in the first place."

"Oh, that's another legal matter. Small claims. We don't handle those issues here. How much does he owe you?"

"About 1000 so far. That's two months rent," said Agatha.

"Sounds like trying to get the money from the neighbor is like squeezing blood from a turnip. Why don't you shut the electricity off?"

Was she serious?

When Agatha was a little girl, she was scared of the dark, and always checked her closet and under her bed for monsters.

Her small bedroom in the Bronx included a cot, a bookshelf full of books, and a small desk. Agatha loved the desk. She liked writing stories, and reading books. Books were her best friends. After she went to the Bronx Zoo, she started reading about animals, especially hippos. She thought about Baby Odin and hoped he wasn't lonely and sad anymore.

Instead of pop star posters, her bedroom included Greek Orthodox icons that were inside a glass wooden case that hung off her puce colored wall. There were images of Jesus on the cross, Jesus as a baby staring up at his mother, St. John the Baptist, St. Spyridon, St. Eleftherios, St. Mary of Egypt, and the Virgin Mary in her tomb. Besides the icons, there was a hanging gold plated oil lamp that her mother often lit at night. The light comforted her, but when it burnt out, the streetlamps outside their house cast ominous shadows on the icons, and she was afraid to look at Jesus on the cross. He looked dead. Hanging over the headboard of her bed was a gold cross that had rested on the chest of Great Uncle Gus, as he lay in his coffin. She remembered being at the old man's wake. He was 93 years old when he died. Her mother had lent the cross to his hysterical wife, Great Aunt Vasiliki for the wake. Agatha was haunted for years by the image of the old man's pale white hands, clasped around the cross, against his icy cold chest.

Her mother made her say the Lord's Prayer every night in Greek, in front of those awful icons, even when she did not want to. One time she told her mom that she hated Jesus and that she was happy that Great Uncle Gus had died. In response, her mom slapped her across the face.

Agatha flinched at the end of AA meetings, when all the attendees held hands and said the Lord's Prayer. It never occurred to her that she could keep silent. She muttered the Lords' Prayer, under her breath, in Greek, cringing the whole time.

Shortly after she got the three-day notice, there was a morning when she did not get out of bed, and go to work. This time she did not even bother to call her boss. She just stopped showing up, and a week after she quit, she received a small check which barely covered the cost of food and gas for a week or so.

She continued her dogs' exercise regime. Exercise helped her maintain the little sanity she had left. First she ran with Odin. Then she walked Zelda and Loki, followed by a stroll with Freya and little Layla, a little blonde haired, dachshund mix. Odin was older, and after running for a few minutes, he drooled. She always shared her bottled water with him, and he slurped the liquid happily. Running with Odin on the desert trails made her feel more connected to God, than that stupid Lord's Prayer.

A few weeks after the three-day notice, Agatha received an unlawful detainer notice which meant that she had five days to respond or else she would be out in the streets with her dogs in a matter of days. She called back the legal assistance clinic, and secured the free services of their attorney who asked her to fax over copies of the lease, and rental receipts.

Agatha drove about 12 miles to Staples to Lancaster, as there were no fax services in the Mojave Desert. After she left Staples, she went to a meeting in Palmdale. While she listened to fellow alcoholics sharing their feelings of gratitude, she sank deeper into her seat.

What the hell did she have to be grateful for?

Where was she going to find a home with five dogs?

After the meeting, she spoke with a female oldtimer, and told her about the eviction.

"Maybe you should rehome some of your dogs," the woman said.

When she left the meeting it was about 8:30 pm. On her way home she thought, I should take my sponsor's direction and find homes for the damn dogs. Maybe I should just dump them at the pound! It's hard to find landlords that take pit bulls! I need to do the right thing for once! Take care of me!

When she opened the front door, her mind was racing. She forgot to shut the door behind her. Odin, Loki, Zelda and Freya tore outside like convicts that just broke out of Alcatraz. Layla stayed inside the house, wagging her little tail and yipping. The four pit bulls bolted down the porch, and ran out of the unfenced yard, into a dirt road, which lead to Backus Road, the main street by her house.

"Damn it!" she screamed.

To make things worse, there was the idiotic neighbor driving his oxygen delivery van down the dirt road. He blasted rap music. She ran into the road, calling out her dogs' names. Zelda, Loki and Freya ran back to the house. The neighbor stopped in front of Backus, and made a right turn, with Odin in full chase. Agatha ran towards the road. In a matter of seconds, she was out of breath. But it was too late.

Odin disappeared into pitch-black darkness.

Her heart crumbled like a piñata that had just been smashed.

When she got to the main road, he was gone.

After Agatha ran back to her house, making sure that the other dogs were safe, she jumped into her Ford Escape. She drove into the direction where she last saw Odin. Since the darkness was overpowering, she turned on her high beams. She rolled down her windows and screamed, "Odin!" The wind swallowed her cries.

In the darkness, she heard coyotes screaming.

She aimlessly drove around in the desert. There was no sign of Odin, and her heart sank. She had to keep going. She could not stop. She had to keep looking. Even if she died in the process, she could not stop. While she searched for her dog, her heart cried out, where are you?

Since her gas tank was almost empty, she drove to the gas station in Mojave. Even though she had half a pack of cigarettes, she bought another pack.

After she bought gas, she drove to Stater Brothers.

What a sight she was, wearing cut off jean shorts, dirty sneakers, and an old Nirvana t-shirt that had a hole in it. Her armpits were covered with sweat. Agatha's hair was propped on top of her head, like a bunch of dead weeds, barely held together with a hair claw. Strands of hair covered her eyes, but she was too tired to brush them away.

The supermarket was about to close.

She grabbed a shopping cart, and rolled it over to the liquor aisle.

She saw a bottle of Merlot. As she picked up the bottle, a chill went through her bones. The wine looked like blood! Hurriedly, she shoved the bottle back on the shelf. She saw a bottle of chardonnay, but damn it, the wine looked like urine.

What about vodka? I know how to make a damn good Woo Woo, she thought.

Agatha rolled the shopping cart over to the hard liquor, which was inside a glass case. As she caught a glimpse of her reflection, she almost jumped out of her skin. She looked like Kayako's ghost from *The Grudge.*

And she felt just as dead.

She gaped at a bottle of Svedka. The bottle looked like a cremation urn that she saw online. Was that where her remains were going to end up? Stuck inside an empty bottle of Svedka for eternity?

Over the loudspeaker, a voice said, "Thank you for shopping at Stater Brothers, but the store is now closed. Please bring your final purchases up to the front for checkout. For your convenience, we will be open again tomorrow at 8 am."

She rolled the shopping cart away from the liquor aisle. Her stomach growled. She went over to the deli and grabbed a container of whipped cream cheese. Then, she scurried down another aisle, in search of bagels. Where the hell were the bagels? As she walked by the pet food section, she felt a lump in her throat.

Where the hell is my Odin? Where is he? She thought. Where is my baby?

She wanted to scream, but a clerk rushed over.

"Is there something you are looking for?" he asked.

"Bagels. Where are the bagels?" she asked, trying not to freak out.

He pointed his finger towards an aisle, and she loudly rolled the cart over, like a banshee out of hell. As she stared at the loaves of bread, her vision blurred, and a sensation of lightheadedness came over her. Instead of bagels, she grabbed a loaf of Wonder Bread, and headed over to checkout.

Agatha spent the rest of the night driving, looking for Odin. Finally at three in the morning, she went home, defeated. Instead of excitedly jumping on her, Freya, Layla, Loki and Zelda parted like the Red Sea. They looked sad, especially Loki, her pit bull/lab mix who looked like the large version of a Boston terrier. Usually, his ears perked up, as if they were held up by pipe cleaners, but that morning one of his ears drooped.

Do they know something I don't know? Agatha wondered. Do they sense that something awful might have happened to their brother?

As she walked towards the bathroom, she felt as if she was an undertaker carrying a coffin down the aisle of a church.

Inside the bathroom, she turned the light on and morosely stared at her reflection in the mirror.

Growing up as a kid in the Bronx, everyone around her told her that she looked like her father. He was a good-looking man when he was younger, but when he got older, he just slept all day long, just like she did when she was depressed. Her parents fought a lot, too. Just like the neighbors next door in the Mojave. Just like Agatha and Tom did.

A year before she married Tom, she invited her mother, who had recently underwent a mastectomy, to visit her and Tom in Los Angeles.

"Why the hell is she coming here?" Tom asked. "You told me that all you ate at school were crappy cream cheese sandwiches."

"My mom has cancer," Agatha said.

Agatha and Tom lived in a mansion in Bel Air. He was a B-movie screenwriter, and they both lived off his trust. His own mother had bought the house for him, paid in cash, a year before he met Agatha.

During the visit, Agatha and her mother drove down to Laguna Beach. They had lunch at the Driftwood Kitchen, an oceanfront restaurant with stunning views of the beach. Agatha ordered a glass of pinot grigio, lit a cigarette, and then ordered another glass of wine even though she was still halfway through the first glass.

"Are you happy with him?" Her mother asked in Greek. She hardly spoke any English even though she had been in the United States for decades.

"We're getting married soon," Agatha said. "Do you remember that song by The Turtles? That's going to play when Tom and I dance for the first time as husband and wife."

Her mother shook her head, and said, "You drink and smoke too much."

It was sunrise, when Agatha resumed her search, scouring the area where she and Odin loved to run. The trails were strewn with rocks, and her SUV bounced up and down. She did not have four-wheel drive and the bouncing made her want to vomit. In the distance, she saw a landscape of sand colored mountains covered with red and black rock formations. Clusters of yellow, purple and white flowers provided color to the harsh landscape. A roadrunner sprinted several feet away, darting behind a Joshua tree. Suddenly, she heard a small thud against her bumper.

She stopped the car, and jumped out.

A rabbit lay on the road, trembling for a few seconds, and then it was still.

The rabbit's eyes stared ahead.

Agatha sat down on a rock by a cactus, and stared at the rabbit, and then at the pink cactus flowers, which glowed under a golden hue.

Her mother loved cactus fruit. When she came to visit, they went to Whole Foods on Sepulveda and her mother bought pounds of prickly pears. Her mother also purchased a whole ton of organic food, and stocked the refrigerator with groceries. Tom stayed in his room, for the most part, during her mother's visit, and that made Agatha angry. She didn't say a word even though she wanted to scream. Her mother didn't say a word, but she knew that nothing escaped her mother's eye.

Before she boarded the plane to go back to New York, her mother asked, "Are you sure about this guy?'

"Yes, I love him," said Agatha. "Did I tell you about the song we picked for our wedding dance?"

They hugged. Agatha felt tears pouring down her cheeks.

"Cut down on the cigarettes and wine, ok?" Her mother said.

"TWA flight 254 boarding for JFK," said the airline attendant over a loudspeaker.

"They are calling me," her mother said, as if she were the only passenger on the plane.

As her mother walked away, Agatha said, "I will see you at the wedding!"

That was the last time she ever saw her mother alive.

While Agatha gazed at the dead rabbit, she noticed that her hands shook.

There was no wedding. There was no first sappy dance as husband and wife. There was no Turtles song. They drove to Vegas and Tom listened to Pink Floyd all the way to Nevada. Agatha hated Pink Floyd, but she didn't say anything. After they eloped in Vegas, the fighting got worse. She was the ultimate Bel Air housewife, without the fringe benefits. When her father died from a heart attack, Tom refused to buy her a plane ticket to go to the funeral back east. One night, Tom lost his temper, punched her in the face and gave her a black eye. After she finally left, he froze all the credit cards and she was left with an old Ford Explorer and the shirt on her back and an old hair dryer that didn't work. After they went to court, she was awarded a little alimony, but it was not enough. Because they had only been married for a short time, plus the fact that they lived off his trusts, she became a pauper. Like a stray dog in search of shelter, she moved from motel to motel. Shepicked up restaurant and bar jobs here and there. Sometimes she called her mother, drunk, screaming for money. Oddly, her mother did not get mad at her. She just sounded very tired on the phone. And she always sent Agatha a little money, even though one time her sister, Evadne picked up the phone, and said, "You should be ashamed of yourself, asking ma for money! Her cancer is back."

"I hope she dies," said Agatha, and hung up.

After that, she could not bring herself to call her mom anymore.

One night, Agatha was sitting on a bench on Skid Row, drinking cheap brandy mixed with diet coke, and smoking a cigarette. The liquor helped with the loneliness, and the cigs kept her awake. In the distance, she saw a woman walking a blue nosed pit bull. Maybe that's what she needed! A dog! Suddenly, her cell phone rang. It was her sister, Evadne.

"You need to come home," Evadne said. "Mama wants to see you."

"Why?" Agatha asked, slurring her words.

"You're drunk," her sister asked.

"No, I am not drunk," Agatha said. "What does she want?"

"She is dying," Evadne said.

"Oh, my God," said Agatha.

Suddenly, a hummingbird appeared. It buzzed around a pink cactus flower, and danced up and down like music notes from a Beethoven sonata. Agatha looked into the distance, and against the sandy colored mountain, she thought she saw Odin, but it wasn't Odin, it was just shadows against a rock. As the sun rose higher in the sky, the shadows elongated and moved, and one shadow looked like a woman in the distance, and she thought she heard a familiar female voice, speak in Greek. Or maybe it was just the wind.

Agatha hopped back into her car. Instead of retracing familiar routes that she took with Odin, she drove west on Backus Road.

A feeling of exhaustion came over her, as if she were on that plane landing at JFK, in New York City, so long ago. Evadne and her brother-in-law Stavros picked her up at the terminal. Before she could thank them for buying her a plane ticket, Evadne said, "Mama died two hours ago."

Agatha felt as if ice had shot up through her veins, like embalming fluid.

At the wake, her mother lay in an open casket. Her mother had a bitter expression on her cream colored face. There was the gold cross, that same gold cross that had haunted Agatha as a child, clasped between her dead cold hands. Her nails were painted lavender, too, but Agatha just gazed at the cross.

After the funeral, Evadne told Agatha that their mother had removed her from the will, three days before she died. Agatha hid her anger, by pouring herself a glass of wine, drinking it rapidly, muttering, "I don't care. I don't care."

Evadne and Stavros deserved the townhouse on Corlear Avenue in Kingsbridge. They paid for everything, including her mother's medical expenses, and of course, the funeral arrangements. Even though her mother had stage four cancer at the time of her diagnosis, she lived for over six years. But why did her mother include her worthless younger brother, Evan in her will? Why was Agatha left out? She didn't really care about living in that damn house, and sensed that Evan would probably sue Evadne for his share of the house, but being left out of the will eradicated any love she had felt for her mother.

Evadne presented Agatha with legal papers appointing herself as executor of the estate. Agatha poured herself a shot of ouzo, and took a swig, feeling the dry anise flavored liquor burn her throat. Blindly, she signed the papers. And then after four shots of ouzo, Agatha began screaming at Evadne. Then, she went into a blackout. When she woke up, she was on a flight back to Los Angeles, which made no sense because her visit was supposed to last for two weeks. After her mother passed away, Agatha never went back to the Bronx.

As she drove down Backus Road, she absentmindedly wondered if the cross, had been buried with her mother or had Evadne kept it as a memento? Who called the airlines bumping her flight up to the day after the funeral? How could Evadne and Stavros let her fly back to Los Angeles in a black out?

Suddenly, Agatha saw a dog, covered with dirt, trudging east, on the side of the road.

Her heart skipped!

Was that Odin?

Agatha made a U-turn, and pulled up beside the gray figure, which stopped moving. She jumped out of the car, ran over and saw that the figure was not Odin, but only an empty black trash bag that ballooned with the wind. It flailed noisily against a bunch of weeds, like a toothless person flapping his gums.

Agatha screamed, "Odin! Odin!"

She thought she heard a bark.

Frantically, she wiped dirt away from her face. A few specks had gotten into her eyes, and she could feel her contact lenses drying up. But there he was, across the street, trudging east. He was caked with mud, and drool dripped from his mouth. Hunched over, he kept moving forward, one step at a time. He had a sense of purpose, as if he knew the path home. Despite all the danger surrounding him, racing cars, trucks and Bobcats hiding out in the desert, he kept moving forward.

"Odin!"

He stopped, and turned his head.

He saw her.

"Odin!" she yelled, feeling tears of joy streaming down her face.

He stood there waiting.

Suddenly, she heard a song blaring from a car. For a moment, she felt confused as she heard, "Imagine me and you, I do."

It was an old hearse that stopped in the middle of the street. The hearse blocked her view of Odin. Agatha bolted, running around the car's trunk. She had to get to her dog!

"Hey!" The driver yelled, while that damn song kept playing. "Hey!"

After she crossed the street, Odin was gone!

Confused, she heard the sound of the hearse driving off, with the song fading off into the distance. Then she saw the dog running towards an old abandoned shed. She chased him, fighting the heavy gust of wind that threatened to blow her over. One of her contact lenses fell out of her eyes. Blinded, she stumbled over a cactus and fell flat on her face.

When she looked up, covered with scrapes, dirt and blood, she saw the dog several feet away, staring at her. The mud was gone and she saw the dog's face.

It was a stray pit bull, one of many that roamed the desert, one that might have been dumped by pitiless owners, many who purchased pitbull puppies from backyard breeders, raised them and then after realizing that the dogs were no longer cute babies dumped them heartlessly in the middle of the Mojave. And of course, some of these dogs ended up at the pound, where they had no chance.

The dog gave her a look of pity, and then he bolted away, running towards a dilapidated shed, where a terrier with matted hair waited, wagging its tail.

Heading back towards her car, Agatha stumbled over tumbleweeds, and purple wildflowers. She stepped on the skeletal remains of a dead cat or was it a dead dog? Prick corns got into her bare legs and she winced. She tripped over rocks, and dead branches from Joshua trees. Tears came to her eyes, and the other contact lens that precariously hung on became moistened so that she could at least clearly see from one eye.

When she got back to her car, she leaned against the hood, trembling. She had no idea what she was going to do next.

Judging from the position of the sun, Agatha estimated the time to be about nine am. She had an image of Odin stumbling around the desert, drooling from lack of water. Or had animal control picked him up? But did they drive around looking for stray dogs during the evening? Had he gone up to some peoples' property, chased their chickens and had been shot? Even though he had an identification tag, people tended to keep their distance from him.

In her heart, she knew that he was lost and desperately trying to find his way home.

The despair that made her heart pound, while tears poured down her face, paralleled the grief that the baby hippo had felt so many years ago, upon losing his mother. She flailed her arms in the sky, and wailed.

Funeral Preparations for Mr. Cromwell D. Scone, God Rest His Soul

Darwin Dye, wearing a black tuxedo, leather lace up dress shoes, a crisp white shirt and a black satin tie placed the finishing touches on the deceased. He polished the coffin with Lemon Fresh Pledge. After Dye applied rouge to the withered cheeks of Mr. Cromwell D. Scone, he inserted newspaper inside the body's tuxedo pants. Dye rolled up Scone's tuxedo sleeve to reveal a diamond studded Rolex. He peered at the watch, before pulling down the sleeve, hiding the timepiece from view.

"Any relation to the deceased?" Dye asked.

"Business associate," I said.

"Do you own a Rolex too?" he asked.

I remained silent.

"Aha!" Dye said, before he inserted a gold cross between Scone's folded hands. As he arranged wreaths, brimming with red, white, and pink roses, lilies, hydrangeas, baby's breath and funeral ribbon sayings, I looked around the parlor. There were five rows of red velvet chairs, separated by an aisle. A crystal chandelier, as well as two floor lamps provided dim light. I walked over to a cherry wood pulpit, which held a guest book, along with a stack of prayer cards, which depicted Jesus welcoming a photo-shopped Scone ghost into heaven. On the back of the card, were the words, *Dye Funeral Home*. Suddenly, Dye began to hum under his breath. “Fiddle Diddle Dee, where’s my pot of gold? I am a leprechaun and I never get old.”

Much to my horror, I watched as he skipped around the coffin, clapping his hands.

A Winter Coat

On a nightstand, there were red roses in a glass vase. Against the hospital's stark fluorescent lighting, the roses made Calliope's eyes hurt. That night, after she landed at JFK a cab drove her straight to the hospital.

Eyes closed, he lay on the hospital bed, and breathed through an oxygen mask. Tubes and catheters stemmed out of his nose and arm. The heart monitor's screen showed spiked lines. On the top right, there were two numbers, one over the other. A pulse oximeter was attached to his finger.

Like a bumblebee, a nurse buzzed around his bed.

"Who brought the roses?" Calliope asked.

"I don't know," the nurse said.

"My husband bought me roses when we met."

The nurse smiled and left the room.

Calliope walked over to the nightstand, where the flowers perched, like soldiers at attention. She touched a rose. A few petals cascaded to the floor. Suddenly, he had a coughing fit. Startled, she knocked the vase over. Flowers and water scattered everywhere. The vase shattered into broken shards. She saw her broken reflection in the glass pieces, like a cubist painting by Chagall.

He retched. There was green sputum on his lips. The oxygen mask fell off. The spiked lines on the monitor moved faster. She pressed the emergency button, and then scrambled on the floor, picking up the roses.

The nurse reappeared, like a fairy godmother. After the nurse gave him a shot and adjusted his mask, she saw Calliope hunched over, in a corner, staring at her clenched fist. Blood mixed with the roses, making the flowers look like rust.

The nurse cleaned and bandaged her right hand. An aide swept up the glass. Calliope stared at the man in the bed, who settled into a deep sleep, his chest rising up and down, like the waves she saw outside the Royal Hawaiian's window where Mas and she stayed during their honeymoon in Hawaii, years ago.

"Have to change your father's bedpan," said the nurse.

"I'll go smoke," said Calliope.

"Honey, it's freezing outside," said the nurse. "Where's your coat?"

The woman's kindness took her aback. Calliope shrugged, and picked up the roses from a chair, where she had left them.

As Calliope walked down the hallway, the smell of Pine-sol permeated her senses. Although they lived in a huge house, Mas refused to hire a maid. He made Calliope clean, to earn her keep, and told her that she had to use Pine-Sol to scrub the toilets. The smell made her ill.

Once she reached the parking lot, she hurled the roses into the darkness. She shivered in her thin leather jacket. After she booked the flight, they fought. As usual, the argument was about money. He had millions, and she had none except for the money he gave her, because she was a loser actress, a fact that he threw in her face. He paid for all her needs, from cigarettes to meals to headshots, and even a nose job. Before she left LA, she begged for a winter coat because New York had sub zero temperatures in February, but he said, "No. That ticket cost me an arm and leg!"

They fought just like her parents used to, except her father never hit her mother.

When she was 29, she fled New York. She did not think rationally when she moved to Los Angeles. It was more of a "fight or flight" response. In Hollywood, she got lost like many actors do. It was a town full of beautiful blondes with long legs, driving around in top down convertibles, blasting pop music.

And there was dark-haired, chain-smoking Calliope. She drove an old Chevette and blasted *Metallica* on the radio to cover up the noise inside her head. Although she moved 2451 miles away, she still heard them arguing. The music did not help. After Mas and she started fighting, she found relief in booze and benzos.

Outside the hospital, she reached inside her Prada handbag for her cigarettes, and lighter. She had less than fifty bucks in cash, but she had two credit cards. Mas was the authorized user, but she was a joint cardholder. Should she risk buying a coat? He would see it on the billing statement and freak out.

Her hands shook as she lit a cigarette. Inside her bag, there was a mini bottle of Merlot that she confiscated from the airplane, next to her cell phone and a bottle of Xanax.

"Take only as needed for extreme anxiety," the shrink had said.

My anxiety is always extreme, she thought.

She chased a pill with wine and smoked.

As a train screeched into the station a block away, her phone rang.

It was Mas.

She trampled the cigarette with her shoes.

After the phone stopped ringing, she went inside.

As she waited for the elevator, she envisioned Mas home in their Hollywood Hills yellow stucco art deco house. She checked her cell. It was 11 pm Eastern standard time. Back in LA, it was 8 pm.

Like the goddess Aphrodite, the house once rose out of a sea of pink bougainvilleas and red roses. A month ago, Mas and she fought, again, and he pushed her head against the wall. After he let her go, she ran up to their bedroom, locked the door, and stared out of the window, which overlooked Beachwood canyon. Mas stormed outside with a weed whacker. Like the killer in the Texas Chainsaw Massacre, he attacked the roses and bougainvilleas, until all that was left were amputated stubs. In the distance, she heard the peacocks that belonged to a famous drummer who lived in a castle. The birds screamed. For a split second, Calliope thought the sound came from the flowers that were begging Mas for mercy.

As she stumbled down the hallway, she saw a body covered in a black body bag on a bed inside Room 142. In Room 144, there was a white haired old woman propped up in bed. Blue light from the TV flashed across her face. The old woman stared, right at her, and screeched like the peacocks and the sound effects from the movie *Psycho*. Calliope covered her ears, and bolted towards her father's room.

His chest rattled as if his lungs were full of rocks.

Don't take anything native from Hawaii, Mas had said. No rocks or sand. It will bring us bad luck.

Ok, I won't.

I love you, Calli.

I love you, too, Mas.

Another subway train screeched into the station.

So many years ago, when she lived at home in the Bronx with her parents, she left, five days a week, at 8 am, to take the subway to NYU. One cold winter day, she overslept and left at 8:30 am. She threw on a hoodie, because she couldn't find her coat, and her acting teacher hated tardiness.

As she waited for the train on the outdoor subway platform, she saw her father, carrying a briefcase, wearing his thick winter coat. He walked right by her, keeping his head down, until he became an exclamation point in the distance.

When the train came, he entered a separate car.

Why did she marry Mas? Was it because he was ten years older than her, and represented the father she never had as a child? Or was it because she was out in LA alone and had been for years? First she worked as a cocktail waitress at the Rainbow, and then as a waitress at the Beachwood coffee shop, which was where she met Mas one morning, when he sat at the counter, and she served him pancakes? By then, she had gotten her SAG card, thanks to *THE BLOOD OF THE DAMNED,* an awful B-movie where she played *VAMPIRE'S VICTIM #2.* Speaking two words got her the damn card.

"Help me."

His eyes opened.

"My daughter, take my coat," he said with a smile. "Sit next to me on the train."

She took his cold hand in hers. His lips were blue, and his face was a pale green, but his eyes were brown like hers.

"This time, stay," he said.

"Ok," she said.

He sighed, and closed his eyes.

The nurse came back. While the nurse adjusted his oxygen levels, Calliope pulled her hand away and walked to the window. Outside there was a little girl dressed in red playing in the snow, bobbing up and down, like an apple being dunked in white Belgian chocolate. Her cell phone rang. It was Mas. Her hands trembled as if she held a grenade. Suddenly, the EKG monitor sounded an alarm. Startled, she dropped the phone, while the piercing sound of the alarm drowned out the telephone ring. A crack formed on the screen like a lightning bolt. Nurses ran into the room, and someone yelled, "Code Blue." She blindly turned towards the window. The little girl was stomping in the snow, as a tall man in a winter coat appeared. The child ran towards him, screaming with laughter, as he picked her up, held her in his arms, and carried her away.

Bel Air, 2500

As Martin Lehmann downloaded the Time Traveller App on his iPhone Z, his wife Maria patrolled the room, wringing her hands that revealed artificial silver-colored nails that were ten inches long.

"I can't believe I rescheduled my manicure for this," said Maria.

Ignoring her, Martin opened the app on his phone. Siri spoke. "Please speak or enter the four digit year that you wish to visit."

"2500," said Martin.

"How many time travellers?"

"Two."

Was this a good idea? Maria wondered, as she hugged her leather jacket close to her chest. After all, she had always taken risks. Her fearlessness had been the major building block to her success as CEO of GIRL'S GUISE, a major corporation that provided eternal youth to women with ethereal masks conceived from the faces of dead females. Now she wanted to jump into her Jaguar, and take off. Her idiot husband looked like Elvis Presley as he bopped around the sunlit living room of their French style estate. Maybe this time travel experience could save their marriage. Or maybe she could dump him in the future and return to the present by herself. No such luck. He was the only one who could figure out the damn app.

"Please provide images which are required for transport," said Siri.

Martin grabbed Maria by the waist, and snapped a selfie.

"Scan barcodes," said Siri.

Martin scanned the bar codes that looked like tattoos on his and Maria's wrists.

"This is ridiculous," said Maria.

"Transport installed. Please punch your passcode to return."

Maria and Martin Lehmann of 1919 Bellagio Drive, Bel Air, California disappeared from view. All that was left of the lovely couple was a button, from Maria's jacket, which had fallen onto the white rug.

In the year 2500, the Lehmann's one hundred million dollar mansion had been replaced by a building constructed from blue glass symmetrical cubes. The structure looked like a mathematical puzzle. There was no greenery to be found. There were no luxury cars. The other neighborhood mansions were replicas of the mathematical puzzle. Besides green glass, other colors included pink, yellow, blue and orange. All of Los Angeles was covered with cubes.

"Where the hell is the 405?" said Martin.

Suddenly a mechanical voice spoke out of nowhere.

"Have a wonderful day, Z200 and Z201."

"Can they see us?" Maria whispered.

"The app ensures that we remain invisible."

On the ground floor, a blue door opened. Two figures, both wearing second skin orange outfits labeled, *Z200, Male* and *Z201, Female*, emerged from the house. The outfits covered them completely.

"Orange Spidermen!"said Maria.

Z200 and Z201 lifted the orange material that covered their faces, to reveal contraptions that looked like stainless steel vegetable strainers. Z200 rolled up the right sleeve of his outfit to reveal a bar code on his arm. Then he scanned the code over the front door, which blinked like a siren. Inside the house, there was a loud whooshing sound. The figures nodded, so that their strainers touched. They covered their faces, before dissolving into thin air.

Suddenly, Maria, who felt lightheaded, noticed that Martin's face was blue.

"We're running out of oxygen," she said, gasping for air.

"I can't remember the passcode," Martin said.

"This is all your fault," said Maria.

Martin remembered the passcode.

While he typed the number on his phone's keypad he had an evil thought.

Leaving Maria behind in the year 2500 would be cheaper than a divorce.

Homeless with Six Dogs

The day I officially became homeless was several days before President Trump met Kim Jun Un. I knew that Trump was trying to make relationships with North Korea and the United States amenable, but I secretly prayed that North Korea would unleash a ballistic missile on Reeder Track, the awful meth ridden, pot head neighborhood where the dogs and I had resided for over two years in a blue colored mobile home. I owned six dogs. Bragi, Homer and Plato are pitbulls. Athena is a dobie/pitbull/hound mix who was dumped in a field near my house. She loves to pirouette like a ballerina. Peron, who lived up to his name, is a Chihuahua mix. Evita is a dachshund mix.

I wanted Un to give the orders for the missile to hit Reeder Track after my six dogs and I safely left the neighborhood. But then I realized that a nuclear blast would be catastrophic, extending at least 100 miles past Reeder Track. Needless to say, the major loss of life would be tragic. Plus my canines would become radioactive pets.

So that was not a good idea.

On that fateful Saturday, around 12:30 pm, the landlady's handyman, Aidan, a tall white haired man with whisky breath and a Cockney accent waited for us to leave by the gate of what used to be my house. He was armed with new locks to replace the old ones. He also waited for the sheriffs, and animal control to arrive, or so he said when he had called me from his cell phone right before he arrived. I suspected that he had mentioned the sheriffs and animal control so that he could scare the shit out of me, so that he could get rid of me faster. I had prolonged my stay in that house for as long as I could. What do you do when you and your dogs have nowhere to go?

By the time he showed up, my dogs and I were already in my Ford Escape, parked in my driveway, ready to go. The Escape was crammed with an ice chest, doggy tie outs, canned food, clothing and dry, as well as canned dog food. There were dog bowls and a blanket. My other belongings were in Affordable Storage on Lake Isabella Boulevard in a small five by ten unit that was the size of a large closet. I have lived for over half a century, and my life had been relegated to several plastic bins, all different colors, crammed with second hand clothing, along with a small antique Japanese table. There was also my Asian collection, which included the Japanese Buddha, as well as the laughing Chinese Buddha. Besides the Buddhas, the Asian collection comprised Japanese vases and little geisha doll figurines. I had boxes of books, some chewed up by Athena when she was a puppy. Finally, I had a framed lithograph from Picasso's blue period, *The Tragedy*.

While I, along with my six dogs, drove away, I saw Aidan strolling into the yard, armed with new locks. As I suspected, the sheriffs and animal control did not show up. The landlady really wanted me out of there. Do I blame her? Thanks to my claiming bankruptcy, I lived in that house for over seven months rent-free. I left behind an old Maytag washing machine, a small refrigerator, a microwave oven, an old couch, a small old-fashioned television, a round kitchen table, a dresser and an old mattress with springs popping out of gaps like Slinkys. I forgot a bag full of jeans and shorts, as well as my Donald Duck alarm clock, and an iPhone charger. I had given my jasmine and roses plants away to Darcy, a kindly neighbor who had once been a Jehovah's Witness, but had left the church because, as she said, they were a cult where the elders preyed on little girls. Darcy used to smile and wave at me, while the other neighbors poked fun at me. Now she was inside her house, staring at me from behind closed window blinds. Another neighbor, a thin young woman with painted eyebrows, once told me that I was so "fucking weird." Today she stood in her yard, talking on her cell phone, smoking a cigarette. She completely ignored me. I think that I would have been branded a witch back in 1692 during the Salem Witch Trials. I would have probably been burned at the stake.

The old Maytag that I left behind reminded me of the washing machine that was in our house when I was growing up, a house where my parents fought. I ran away from home a lot, and yet I always went back because once again there was nowhere to go. When I went to NYU, I moved into apartment 4A at the Lenmore Apartment Buildings, 58 East 1st Street, New York, New York 10003. Lenmore had a collection of toilets on the sidewalk, in front of the building. Back in the early eighties, 58 East 1st street was known as the Lower East Side. These days it's the chic East Village. What a joke. Anyway, when I left the Village, and moved to Los Angeles to become a movie star, I did not look behind. My dream of becoming a movie star was another joke.

I did not look behind as my dogs and I drove away from the mobile house where I had lived in for over a year, a mobile house that had the words, FUCK OFF written on the front door.

The dogs and I sought refuge at Kissack Bay, which overlooked Lake Isabella. At night, I parked my SUV between two trees, which provided shade. Next to the two trees was a third tree. While I slept in the driver's seat, the dogs were crammed in the passenger seats or in the trunk. In the morning right about seven am, the sun hitting the windshield blinded me. Startled, I would wake up. After I realized that I was about to face another hellish day, I moved the Escape under the third tree where there was an ample shade. It got to the point where I knew instinctively what time it was by the sun's placement. After I parked the car under the third tree, the dogs and I slept a little more. At around 10 am, after I repositioned the car in between the two trees, I put the four large dogs on tie outs, so it was easy for them to potty. I would walk Evita and Peron alongside the lake so that they could pee and poop. Then I hung out in the car, along with Peron and Evita while Bragi, Homer and Plato were outside on their ties outs under the trees. I turned on the air conditioner because of the intense heat that permeated the inside of the vehicle. When I wasn't staring off into space, and smoking like a maniac, I cried like a woman who lost her family to a fatal plane crash.

Since there were so many trees by the lake, I tied a pillowcase around a dead branch that was a few feet away from the trees. The pillowcase served as a marker. It glowed in the dark.

Like an idiot, I thought that the dogs and I were invisible to the outside world. After all, my Escape was titanium Green. I told my self that the car would be camouflaged under the trees and that no one would notice my dogs or me. That's how weird I became. Or perhaps I was in denial about the whole situation.

I was not religious. But I longed for the Second Coming of Christ where I would see Jesus emerging out of the sky. And like the Book of Revelation said, the eyes of Jesus would flash with fire. On his head there were many crowns, along with a sword coming out of his mouth. And there would be robes dripping with blood. Or maybe I wanted to experience the Second Coming and see Jesus. I felt like people had failed me, and I wanted to connect with God, even though I was a skeptic.

Like Jesus who was baptized in the Jordan River, the lake sprinkled me with green water that was far from holy. Unlike Christ, I emerged from the lake covered with toxic green algae. My short bobbed hair was coated with seaweed. I looked like a sprig of parsley.

Even worse than turning green, was trying to hide from the fishermen. The lake was full of fish. Jesus would have a blast. I didn't.

I hated fish. My mom fried trout, and left the head intact. Often she ate the trout's eyeballs, because she believed that by doing so, she would become Superwoman complete with X-ray vision.

But my mother was far from having super powers.

After a six-year battle with breast cancer, she died in 2002. My sister, Maria inherited the house in the Bronx. She has always argued that the house belonged to her, because she took care of our dying mother, and as a matter of fact, my brother-in-law Gus carried my mother up the stairs from the living room to the bathroom. I deserved nothing because, as she said,

I was drinking nonstop 3000 miles away in Los Angeles. I did nothing to help our mother while Maria did everything, and Gus was a living and breathing wheelchair.

Shortly after I became homeless, Maria sent me a text. "It's not possible for you to come back to the house. You have three fucking dogs. I have a family. We live separate lives."

"How am I going to live in my car during the winter?"

"Its not my fault you are homeless," she says. "Deal with it."

Trying to work on my novel was impossible. I didn't have an electrical outlet to charge up my computer. Once in a while I went to Taco Bell on Lake Isabella Boulevard. I used their Wi-Fi to power up the computer. The worst part was that I had to keep the air conditioner in the car running for the dogs. Not only was I terrified of running into animal control but also all my money went to putting gas in the car, along with purchasing cigarettes. Even though I received disability for my depression, I ran out of money pretty quickly. At Taco Bell, you had to purchase an item from the menu to use the Wi-Fi. The dollar burrito was all I could afford. I asked the associate if the burritos contained lard, and she said no.

A homeless woman, in her late sixties, dressed in torn jeans, dirty sneakers and a ripped Led Zeppelin t-shirt was a permanent fixture at Taco Bell. She sat by the drive-thru just a few feet away from the neon menu. Next to her was a black and white pit bull with sad eyes. They appeared to be homeless. I cried when I first saw them, huddled against the wall, until reality swept over me. I was homeless too.

Finally, I discovered an electric outlet behind the Lake Isabella post office. At night, when the weather was fairly comfortable I drove over there, and rolled the windows down so that the dogs could stay cool. Using the outlet, I charged up my Mac. That took about forty-five minutes. One time, a homeless man with an unshaven beard walked by, talking to himself. But even though the computer gets charged, I couldn't write. No matter how hard I tried I couldn't write. I couldn't do anything. My thoughts spun around and around, jumbled up and distorted, like clothing spinning during the final cycle of a washing machine. Not only did I smoke like a fiend, but also I had no appetite. I sent texts to my sister, my sponsor, and a friend, telling them I wanted to hang myself from a tree, but I couldn't kill myself because my dogs would go to the shelter and probably be euthanized. I wore ripped up t-shirts that had chlorine stains. I only owned two pairs of shorts. I bought a scissor from Dollar General so that I could cut up my jeans and make more shorts. Everyday I checked the weather app on my iPhone. For the most part, during the day times, the weather was over 100 degrees.

John, a man who was well known in the community for helping the homeless, supplied me with dog food. He also gave me a zip lock bag that contained toothpaste, cheap cherry blossom lotion, deodorant soap and a razor but no shaving cream. And he also gave me an old ripped up white towel, along with a black tent. I couldn't figure out how to set the tent up nor did I want to. Instead of giving it back to him, I threw it out.

At night, the lake was jam-packed with four legged flying insects. I bought a citronella candle from Dollar General. The bugs flew into the hot wax, and their screaming put my nerves on edge. I wanted to rip my hair out.

There was a spider web on my dashboard, right behind the steering wheel. When I peered closely, I saw a spider producing silk to construct the web, which was getting larger by the day. At one point, I was tempted to use a tissue to wipe away the web, but then I realized that I would be destroying the spider's home.

Nora, a friend of mine who lived in a camper in Texas paid $700 to transport Peron and Evita to live with her. Besides helping me by fostering the dogs, she sent me money so that I could buy food and cigarettes. I was depressed about sending Peron and Evita to Texas, but I knew that they would be in a good home. On a hot July afternoon, the dogs and I drove up to Bakersfield, where we met the transporter in the parking lot of a Days Inn. When I go to Bakersfield, I become miserable because I believe it is the ugliest city that I have ever seen in my life. As I opened the trunk to grab a plastic bag full of dog food for Peron and Evita, the smell of mold made me gag. The four dogs start barking. A duffel bag, six gallons of water and an old smelly blanket fell onto the parking lot. The transporter eyed the car with disgust. He took a few photographs of me with Peron and Evita. As I handed Evita and Peron over to him, Bragi whimpered. I was too numb to cry. Later, I posted a photo on facebook, and my sister said that she would send me lotion because my face was full of wrinkles. Several days after I posted the photo, I deactivated my stupid Facebook account.

About two weeks after Peron and Evita left, a woman on a thoroughbred, dressed in English attire, came riding by on a trail several yards away from our trees. After she pulled her horse to a halt, she yelled at me. Two little blonde girls riding their horses came to a halt right behind her. They were dressed in Western attire. After I ran up to her, because I couldn't hear a word she said, the little girls stared down at me with loathing. I wore a ripped up AC/DC shirt, dirty jean shorts, and pink flip-flops. The woman and the girls reminded me of a Confederate statue. If I owned a slingshot, I would have knocked them off their horses.

The woman said, "You've been here a while."

"I lost my home," I blurted.

"Life can be hard, at times," she said, looking off into space with a weird look in her eyes. Her horse snorted. The little girls pranced around her, impatiently.

I stared at my feet. My blue colored toenails were filthy.

"It would be awful if animal control came and took your dogs," she said.

I did not reply. Then she, along with the girls, trotted off into the distance. Dirt blew into my face. I felt like the most pathetic person in the world.

That night, I parked my SUV close to the lake, which glowed like a sapphire. There was a full moon. The marshes that emerged from the lake looked like Japanese characters against the sky. A cold mist formed on my windshield. How could that be? It was a humid evening in July. I began to shake from a sudden coldness that swept over me.

After I turned the heater on, still trembling, I grabbed a cigarette out of a pack that jutted out of my cheap Louis Vuitton fake handbag. Bragi, Homer, Plato and Athena snored, huddling under a few blankets donated by Web Recycling. After I noticed that my mini pink Bic lighter ran out of fluid, I discovered some matches in my bag.

After I lit a match, I saw my mother standing a few feet away. Hunched over, against the dark blue landscape, she looked like a model from Picasso's blue period. Was I going crazy? My mother had been dead for over fifteen years. I was married at the time, living in a fancy house on Mulholland Drive. Right before she died, I booked a flight to go back to New York. She wanted to say goodbye to me but that didn't happen. I missed my flight and had to wait several hours for the next flight to JFK, where I transferred planes in Dallas. From DFW, I called my sister who told me that my mom had died at 1:15 am. When I finally saw my mother, she lay in a metallic purple coffin surrounded by wreaths made from sickly sweet smelling carnations.

Before I lit the cigarette, the match blew out.

I grabbed another match, and this time, I lit the damn cigarette. Before I looked the window, to see if she was still there, the car's heater blew the cigarette out.

I turned off the heater, and grabbed another match. When I lit the cigarette, I saw her again, but by now, she walked further into the lake, still hunched over like the woman in the Picasso painting that was in storage.

After she disappeared, the match blew out.

I checked the time on my iPhone. It was 1:15 am.

Welcome to Trona

As Amelia D. Belia and I drove on the 14 Freeway north past Red Rock Canyon, my 95-pound pitbull mastiff mix, Pumpkin Boy, sat upright in the passenger seat of Amelia's 2016 blue Toyota Corolla. The air conditioner blew cold air into my face. It was about 100 degrees out there in the desert. How I wish I lived in Seattle where the average temperature during August was 71 degrees.

Pumpkin Boy stared out the window, with a disapproving look on his face. He wasn't too crazy about driving with Amelia, and neither was I. Amelia D. Belia who referred to herself in the rooms of AA as Amelia D. B., was my sponsor. Amelia knew the Big Book inside out, upside down, right side up, backwards and forwards. Like a cookie jar full of Oreos, Amelia was chock full of AA lingo. Her car bumper was plastered with stickers that read, *One Day At A Time*, *Let Go and Let God*, *To Thine Own Self Be True*, and *God's The Driver, The Drunk's in the Trunk*. A sticker of the stupid AA triangle was plastered on her back windshield.

The triangle read, *Unity. Service. Recovery.*

I found out about a rental in Trona on Craig's List. Trona was a town known for its desolation. Additionally, Trona was a brief stopover for Charles Manson and his followers back in the sixties. Because I could no longer afford the rental in Palmdale that I lived in plus the fact that it was a nightmare trying to find a rental that took breed-restricted dogs, I mentioned the Trona rental to Amelia.

"First step to your dilemma is finding a solution," said Amelia.

I wish I had never mentioned the Trona rental to Amelia.

"You have nothing to lose," she said.

So Amelia offered to drive me up to Trona to see a rental that I had no desire to see, smell, or touch. But Pumpkin Boy and I needed a cheap place to live. And I needed Amelia. There was no way in hell that my old Astrostar van would successfully make the drive to Trona from the Antelope Valley. Plus I had given her forty bucks in gas so that we could make the journey to hell.

After we made a right turn onto Redrock Ransburg Road, I checked out the barren desert landscape. When I was a kid growing up in the Bronx, I loved reading the comic book series, *The Witching Hour*. There was one story where boulders came to life and turned into monsters. I half expected the boulders on Redrock Ransburg Road to transition into demons.

"This is God's country," said Amelia. "Easy to connect with a Higher Power here."

"The only Higher Power you can connect with here is Lucifer," I said, craving a cigarette, but Amelia forbade smoking in her precious Corolla. My mind spun like a teetotum.

I was from the Bronx. How the hell did I end up here? I thought. What the fuck was this? What the hell had I done in a past life to deserve this shit? Who the hell had I been? Maybe Jack the Ripper had an accomplice, named Joan the Ripper? Had I been Joan? The Ripper? And why in God's name was Amelia D. Belia my sponsor? Should I get another sponsor?

Weren't they all crackpots? Maybe I should throw Amelia out of the car, drive off with Pumpkin Boy, and head to Ridgecrest where I could find a liquor store, book a room at a cheap motel, lose my sobriety, drink a gallon of wine, and die, only to be found by a housecleaner the next day.

Suddenly, I couldn't breathe. I was having a panic attack.

I grabbed a prescription bottle from my fake Prada handbag. I popped a Valium, followed by a gulp of my Diet Coke, which naturally had gotten warm despite the cold air from the air conditioner that blasted into my face. Amelia sniffed, like a bloodhound hunting ducks. Or maybe she had eyes on the side of her head like a halibut. As we drove on State Route 178, she said, "Aha!"

"Breath mint," I said.

"Hmmm," she said.

Who the hell was she? Nurse Ratchet?

"Valium!" I said.

"Benzodiazepine," she said.

Couldn't she just say benzo?

"Prescribed. Take as needed. And I need it," I said.

"Addict in recovery plus benzodiazepine. Danger! Danger!" she said, sounding like the robot from *Lost in Space*, a TV show that unfortunately was a milestone during my youth.

"And acid is a hallucinogen," I say.

"What are you talking about?"

"Amelia, you of all people, should know this. Bill W. along with Aldous Huxley, author of the apocalyptic novel, *Brave New World*, partook in LSD experiments during the 1950s for his depression," I said. I was a snob but so what.

"Benzodiazepines are highly addictive," she said.

AA people hate negative talk about AA co-founder and god like figure Bill Wilson. While legal at the time, Bill W.

popped a little acid here and there. He hallucinated just like I did during the only time I took acid. I was about twenty.

For hours, I stood like a lamppost, bent over like the Hunchback of Notre Dame, in my sister's living room in Boston staring at a vase full of dried purple flowers. When I touched the petals, streaks of purple flickered in the air like shooting stars. "Wow," I muttered, "Wow." When my sister came home, she moved my catatonic body to the couch. I told her to go fuck herself.

Maybe some of the AA morons didn't know about the experiments. If they did, most of the AA idiots had no idea who Aldous Huxley was. As a matter of fact, when I mentioned the LSD experiments and Huxley at meetings, I saw the faces of those sober fools go blank. And when they shared, they changed the subject. Which is exactly what Amelia D. Belia did.

"Resentments are our number one offenders," she said. "Do you have a resentment against me?"

Pumpkin Boy growled.

"Pumpkin Boy has a resentment against me. Maybe he needs to work the steps. May the higher power force be with you, Pumpkin Boy," she said, breaking into hysterical laughter as if that idiotic comment was the funniest thing in the world.

When we arrived to the outskirts of Trona, a white sign with a crooked red cross perched on top like a rooster on a weather announced in black letters, OUR CHURCHES. The sign included a list of nine churches.

"Where there's churches, there are a plethora of AA meetings!" Amelia said.

Shut up, Amelia D. Belia, I thought. Shut the fuck up.

Most of the houses in the neighborhood were boarded up, deserted or charred. Some had smashed-in windows. I thought I saw a few skeletons staring at me from a window but I attributed it to the intense desert heat and Amelia's 12-step ranting. Dominating the desolate landscape was the Searles Valley Minerals, Inc. Chemical Plant, which produced borax, salt, soda ash, boric acid and salt cake. The plant spewed noxious white smoke into the air. There was a sulfur-like stench.

"Asbestos," I whispered under my breath.

"By the time you get cancer, you'll be skating on ice in a cemetery heading to an open grave," Amelia D. Belia said.

If only I could whack her on the head with her stupid Big Book, fourth edition, which was perched on her dashboard. If I could hit her hard on the head, maybe she would get a concussion.

Tenants slowly emerged from their houses to check us out. They looked like extras from *The Walking Dead*. All I got were piercing stares, the kind you get on October 31st from the ugly glowing green eyes of Halloween witches, skeletons and ghost decorations hanging off the doors of houses in sappy suburban neighborhoods.

"This is horrible," I said.

"Its either this or living in your Astrovan," she says, with a smirk.

"Astrostar," I said.

"Same thing," she said.

Maybe one of these zombies would jump on Amelia and chomp her up like a bag of chips.

Mike McGee, the landlord's tall balding handyman who lived in Trona waited for us outside a dilapidated house that had weeds covering the entire pave way like an outburst of acne. A wooden fence surrounding the house looked chewed up as if gophers had gathered into a group, got drunk and had a dinner party. There were boarded up windows. Mike

McGee's face was as red as a Bloody Mary. While it was boiling hot like the depths of Hades, the guy wore a checkered jacket, work boots, and dirty jeans.

"Welcome to Trona," he said. "First time here?"

What was hiding behind his checkered jacket? A chainsaw?

I lit a cigarette.

"Yes. This is our first time ever in Trona, California," said Amelia. "What a lovely place. What a lovely place."

"We're a small town, but we got character. You ladies get a chance to check out the Pinnacles?"

"The what?" I asked, smoking furiously.

"Lots of rocks," Mike McGee said. "Mountains, mud. Calcium carbonate."

"Not yet," I said.

"Is your dog friendly?" he asked, staring at Pumpkin Boy with a slightly nervous look.

Pumpkin Boy barked at him.

"He hates men," Amelia said.

McGee smiled.

Take as needed. Where was my Valium? Shit. I left my fake Prada handbag in the car, I thought.

"House is big enough where you can stick him in one of the rooms if I gotta do repairs" said McGee.

"Pumpkin Boy, you get to have your own bedroom," said Amelia, as she petted him.

For a moment, there was an uncomfortable silence.

"Nothing beats a cold one after a hard day's work," Bobby Boy finally said, as he reached into the pocket of his checkered shirt, and pulled out a Bud. While he popped open the can, Amelia cringed.

"There are other ways to relax at the end of a hard day's work," said Amelia. "Have you tried mindfulness?"

"I'm mindful enough to know when to mind my own business!" he said.

Amelia was taken aback.

"My goodness, I thought you had a limited vocabulary!" she said.

He gave Amelia a piercing stare. At that moment, I really wish he had a chainsaw.

"Lets check out the house," he said.

All of us, including Pumpkin Boy, followed McGee through the front door, which was shaped like a coffin from the 1800's. Since the windows were boarded, I sweated profusely.

Amelia looked excited, as she bounced from room to room like an elf on Christmas Eve. Even though I was about to head into cardiac arrest, I followed her. The house was indeed, huge. There were about five rooms, not including the kitchen and a bathroom that had an old-fashioned white tub with claws. The bathroom walls were covered with blue and white art deco tiles.

"Thera, this room can be your meditation room," she said, twirling around in a room that had Victorian style windows, yellow walls, blue floors and an orange ceiling.

"More like an electrocution room," I said.

Ignoring me, she proceeded into another room. I quickly peeked at the living room where Pumpkin Boy had trapped McGee into a corner. Pumpkin Boy sat perfectly still, staring at McGee who sipped his beer, while he nervously wiped sweat away from his brow.

"Pumpkin Boy, come," I said. Obediently, my fur baby followed me, as I found Amelia inside a gloomy room which was completely painted black, including the boarded up windows."The darkroom," she whispered, as if she had just located the Holy Grail.

I had to admit. The small room was perfect for a darkroom, which I had wanted for years. And she knew that.

"God does for us what we can't do for ourselves" she said, maniacally snapping photos of the room with her iPhone. "But let me ensure that this room will suit your creative needs." Pumpkin Boy hung out with Amelia, as she pulled out a measuring tape and she began measuring the width and height of the room.

I went back into the living room where McGee gulped the last of his beer.

"So who lived here before?" I asked.

"She was about your age, may she rest in peace," he said.

"My God," I said, instinctively crossing myself like a pious Greek Orthodox.

"Single lady. Lonely. Middle-aged. You remind of her. But she had no pets, not even a damn goldfish. Poor thing choked on a glazed donut."

"Oh, my God," I said, still crossing myself.

"Found the body next day later when I came by to fix her porch door. She'd been complaining saying it wouldn't shut right," he said.

"How can someone choke on a glazed donut?" I asked.

"Took out her dentures. Found them on the dining room table," he said.

"Well, she must have had an unusual eye for decoration," I said. "The colors of the room are unique."

"She was colorblind," he said. "I was gonna repaint but landlady figured she would just knock down the rent."

"So someone died in here," I said. "Is that another reason the rent is only 400 a month?"

"Well, it wasn't like the Menendez boys house. This here was an all natural departure from this here world."

Out of the corner of my eye, I noticed Amelia strolling over to the 1950's style kitchen, which included an old fashioned stove, a 1960s yellow formica table, matching chairs and a black and white tiled floor.

Amelia turned on the sink faucets. No water.

"The water's not included?" she asked.

"Searles Domestic Water Company," Mike McGee offered.

"Hmmm," she said.

Amelia turned on a switch.

Nothing.

"Electricity?" she asked, her face turning red. Her head looked like a boiling tea kettle. I could imagine steam surging out of her ears.

"Call Edison. And for gas, there is PG&G," said Mike McGee, as he pulled out another beer from the inside of his jacket.

"No service," said Amelia, pointing to her phone as if she was a kindergarten teacher indicating to a blackboard, showing toddlers that two plus two did not equal five.

I checked my phone. My Sprint phone had no service. Oh my God, what now? Not only could I not make a phone call or use the Internet, but what if I had to call 911 if I was choking to death on a glazed donut? But how the hell would I be able to talk with a donut stuck in my esophagus? I would probably die. I had a complete set of teeth but you never knew. And then to make things worse, what if the neighbors discovered that I was dead? What if they entered this Godforsaken domicile, shot Pumpkin Boy, raided the house like those crazy Cretans did to the widow's home in Zorba the Greek?

"I don't have a phone signal either," I told McGee. "And I have Sprint."

"AT & T," said Amelia.

"Verizon," McGee said. "Nothing else works."

"Is there anything I need to know about this place?" I asked.

An uncomfortable look crossed over his face.

"You ever heard of the Manson family?"

Not only did we get lost and end up in Tehachapi on the way back but I had a major anxiety attack about how

uncool it would be to put "Lives in Trona, CA" on my Facebook profile. I would have to deactivate my goddamn Facebook account. Oh, my God. Once upon a time, my Facebook profile announced to the world that I lived in Los Angeles, California. After I started drinking and moved up to Palmdale in a blackout I changed my place of residence to Palmdale, California. As if that wasn't bad enough. Now Trona?

As Pumpkin Boy snored in the back seat, I swallowed another Valium.

"Hand me one of those," said Amelia, reaching out her hand.

Jellyfish

Out of the blue, a guy I dated shortly, who I met online on a dating site fifteen years ago calls.

Let's just call him Neptune.

In astrology, Neptune is the planet of confusion, illusion and delusion.

Let's make this man unique, although in the scheme of my life, he turned out to be like any other man that I have met in. In the end, he did not love me and told me so.

And that hurt.

But let's be honest. About fifteen years ago, while I was going through a divorce, the last thing I should have done was to date a man. I should have focused on getting my life in order but instead I settled for five-minute tumbles under a comforter on top of a hard futon of a small $500 a month studio apartment in Santa Monica, with two surfboards propped against the walls. The studio smelled of potpourri oil and clean laundry. His bathroom door, a small white tiled room with a miniature white sink, medicine cabinet, and shower could have had a wooden plaque with the word, Bachelor embedded with black magic marker. I remember drinking glass after glass of Chardonnay, while he had been sober for 15 years. I felt sorry for him because he did not drink. I felt sorry for him because he went to AA, which was a cult full of weirdos.

Back then, I was a sucker for punishment.

And he dumped me because I kept calling him. He called me a stalker.

Fifteen years later, he calls.

He found me on my Facebook, sent me a friend request, which I accepted, because I am like an amoeba. I have no boundaries. I felt that I had to allow him back into my life. When I was heavily drinking, after my divorce, and I met some dude, and they wanted to have sex which most of them did, of course, I went along with it, as long as I was drunk. I felt like I owed them something even though honestly, they never were there for me except for meaningless sex, which felt more like a work out at the YMCA. Instead of a nice dinner at a real restaurant, they took me to Denny's. I think I have eaten at every Denny's in Los Angeles. Since Denny's does not serve booze, I often brought along my own concoction. A brandy and diet coke mixer in a diet coke bottle.

After Neptune sent me an instant message on Facebook, I messaged my phone number to him. I didn't want to but I did because I felt like I owed him something, God knows what. Two seconds later, the phone rang and there he was, talking to me, after 15 years as if time had stood still.

I became wary.

I have been sober for six years.

What does he want? Is this just a nice phone call from a long lost friend or was he trying to make amends for dumping me? I was the one who should make amends, considering that I slept with his friend, a few months after he dumped me. I slept with his friend for money, which is pretty sick but that's how it was. I had no cash at the time, because my ex husband had screwed me over. Neptune and I talked for a bit. He was still sober, as a matter of fact, God bless him and thanks to AA, he had 30 years of sobriety. I told him that I had been sober for six years.

He told me that he is happy to hear that I am sober. Then, he shared a ridiculous story about his drinking, something about surfing after drinking a bottle of vodka and almost drowning, and losing his life to the ocean. Why was he telling me this story? Perhaps he was trying to share some sober wisdom. After we talked for an hour, he asked, “You don’t go to AA meetings do you?”

I changed the subject. I asked him if he had another cat, because after all, it’s been 15 years. Sheba or whatever the hell his cat’s name was probably died some time ago. Since cats have nine lives, perhaps the feline was purring on his lap.

“I have a dog. He’s in the ER at the vet. Something’s wrong with his stomach.”

“Hey I can drive down to Santa Monica if you need company. I would lose my mind if my dog was in the ER.” I blurted out like a fool.

“No thank you,” he said.

That was it.

Then he hung up.

An hour later, I checked his wall on Facebook. He had defriended me.

When women reached a certain age, they are advised to not wear eye makeup, because eye shadow emphasized the creases on the eyelids. It’s also a good idea to wear lipstick that matched your gums. Sometimes I stared at my bathroom mirror, while I pulled my lips back, to see what color my gums were. I thought puce lipstick would work.

I didn’t know why we were having a conversation. I was not the same woman I was years ago, a lost soul who found instant gratification in sharing another man's bed, even though deep down inside, I wanted to go back to my beautiful home in the Hollywood Hills, but it wasn't my home any more, it belonged to my ex husband, Kaito whose snobbish mother had bought him the house a year before he met me. While Kaito was a B-movie screenwriter, he mainly survived off the trust fund money that his mother doled to him on a monthly basis. Apparently, his deceased father had put the money in his mother's name.

When we were married, the house's exterior was comprised of green wood. After we got married, he had workers stucco the house with pink, because it was my favorite color.

Then the fights began.

One time he was screaming at me, telling me to leave his house. I could hear my son Jeremy crying over the baby monitors. I ran into his room, where he was leaning against the frame of the crib wailing. I picked him up, and sat in the rocking chair holding him tightly, singing in a cracked voice, "You are my sunshine."

If I knew then, what I know now.

But I didn't know then.

When money is tied up in trusts, it's hard to get a decent settlement. While I had custody, his Beverly Hills attorneys, a husband and wife team named Schneider and Schneider told him that sooner or later, he would get custody of our son, because as they said, "Your ex wife is so messed up, she can't even flip a burger at Burger King."

Like seers from a Greek tragedy, their prediction turned out to be true. He received custody of our son, who I barely saw because I was struggling, financially, emotionally or physically. I was Sisyphus pushing the rock up a hill, only to have it roll back down and crash on me. There is nothing worse than being a non-custodial mom. At the private school that Jeremy attended in Sherman Oaks, the other parents looked down on me as if I were a homeless person. Many drove high end luxury cars, and the few times I drove over there to pick up my son in my cheap T-bird, I received scathing looks. And Kaito once told me that his friends thought I was a loser as a mother. Instead of fighting for my son, I ended up in an abusive relationship with a longhaired man who dressed like a grunge rocker. And I drank. I became the loneliest person in the world.

While my son grew up in the Hollywood Hills, the stucco of the house was transformed from pink to gray, like the color of the sky before a huge thunderstorm hits. Meanwhile, I was renting hovels in Palmdale, followed by the Mojave Desert and finally Lake Isabella. I was as broken as the window that got shattered in my house in Palmdale, when a bunch of kids hurled some rocks over the gated fence.

When I drank around Neptune, he never said anything. He just watched me drink wine, which I poured into an old tin cup that he purchased for ten cents from the swap meet in Bodfish where he owned a cheap mobile house that he had purchased for $20,000. He took me up to Bodfish a few times. And in Santa Monica, I used an empty Starbucks coffee container to drink my wine because he was too lazy to wash dishes. In Bodfish, I washed the tin cup with cold water, because he was too cheap to buy propane. After I dried the cup, I sat it on a dish rack, while the rest of his dishes and cups and utensils and pots and pans remained in the sink, covered with greasy food.

When we met, he owned the studio in Santa Monica. Back then he had a small yard, Sheba the cat and one white senior husky named Sasha. While Sasha had been dead for so many years now, he now owned an Australian Shepherd. That's right. One dog. I had ten.Besides losing Sasha, he traded the studio for a Mediterranean style villa in Mar Vista, which he inherited from his parents. While he still owned the house in Bodfish, he also had acquired a boat, a brand new Toyota Tacoma, a house in Akron, a house in Dallas plus his own electric company. Every five minutes he posted on Facebook. I knew that he had sushi for dinner, last night and the night before and the night before that. I also knew that he went to Venice gym at least once a day and worked out. He loved posting old MTV videos with heavy metal bands. And he voted for Trump.

Years ago, he had promised that he would teach me how to surf. He never did.

He reached out to me after all these years only to reject me again. I felt like an idiot.

For one split moment, Neptune emerged from his mysterious home inside the sea. He was so far away in the distance. I stared at him from the shore, but all I could see was a head attached to a green wetsuit, balanced on a blue surfboard. There was an evil side of me that wished that he would fall into the ocean where he would be devoured by a large jellyfish.

Desperately seeking Xanax Due to Severe Anxiety As Inflicted by Yucca Brevifolia

At her sponsor's suggestion, Alethea dragged herself with the rapidity of a hermit crab to AA meetings three times a week in the Antelope Valley Desert, a place that unfortunately, she called home. Even though her sponsor said that AA was supposed to keep her sober, 12-step meetings drove her nuts. If anything, they made her want to drink. While she was a private person, she noticed that alcoholics loved talking about themselves. Even though they were supposed to share their experiences, strengths and hopes, many of them got fixed on their experiences, often sharing about their drinking days for what appeared to be an eternity, even though they were supposed to limit their shares between three and five minutes.

Alethea was at the 7:30 pm WE TRULY CARE meeting, which took place inside a dump on Avenue D and Sierra Highway, in Lancaster. The place was once a bar, and had been converted to a meeting hall. On the wall, an old BUD sign had been refurbished to read, BUDDIES OF BILL. There were still bar stools. Instead of drunken patrons' butts sitting on the stools, the stools were covered with AA literature. When the hall first opened, there were ashtrays on the bar. Now members smoked outside during the break, sipping coffee that tasted like Echinacea. There were plastic picnic tables along with plastic chairs crammed in the room. Alethea sat on a cheap plastic chair in the back.

At the podium, Joshua, a recovering alcoholic shared his goddamn experience, strength and hope. Alethea checked the industrial clock on the wall. So far, Joshua had rambled for over twenty minutes.

"After I got my second DUI twenty-seven years ago, judge sent me to AA. I didn't want to come here, and be with you fools. I remember this cute blond who thirteenth stepped me. I didn't do it. I only did the first twelve," Joshua said.

As the members in the room laughed, Alethea wanted to throw up. The entire group stared at Joshua, as if they were members of the Heaven's Gate cult, and he was their demented leader, Marshall Applewaite.

Desperately trying to divert her attention, Alethea gazed at the wooden plaques hanging off the walls. Each plaque was engraved with a tasteless AA cliché, along with the recovering alcoholic's first name, followed by the first initial of their last name (to preserve anonymity, even though every one knew that most alcoholics were serious gossips). The plaques included the recovering alcoholic's sobriety date. She located Joshua's plaque. STICK THE PLUG IN THE JUG, JOSHUA D., JANUARY 5, 1980.

Cover your mug with the jug, Joshua, she thought.

As she gagged while she sipped the God awful coffee from a Styrofoam cup, she noticed that Cremora floated on the surface of the lukewarm liquid, coagulating into weird little forms.

One of the shapes looked like California, a state that she had moved to years ago from New York City, when she was young and full of dreams. She had moved to Los Angeles to become a famous screenwriter. Unlike the Cremora, that dream evaporated many moons ago.

Instead of the pink bougainvilleas that beautified the Palisades home that she once lived in with her husband, she now resided in the Mojave Desert, surrounded by a plant species known as Yucca Brevifolia, commonly known as Joshua Trees. After a divorce, HE got the house and the Ferrari and she ended up with nothing more than the clothing on her back, a Ford Explorer with a leaky radiator and a sudden urge to drown her misery with cheap Chardonnay. A few years later, she met abusive husband number two. He drank, too, but never owned up to it. He nicknamed Althea the "whore" and the "drunk." After they got evicted from their cabin in the Los Angeles National Forest, they ended up in the Antelope Valley Desert. When he walked out on her one day in 2007 to hook up with a secret girlfriend in Santa Fe, leaving her with a house that had no electricity, thanks to nonpayment of the bill, she was still drinking cheap Chardonnay, getting sloshed like a paper boat floating in a swamp.

That was over ten years ago.

"Just sit right back, And you'll hear a tale, A tale of a fateful trip," Joshua sang the opening lyrics from the *Gilligan's Island* theme. The AA's burst into laughter. Alethea wanted to bolt out of the room but she was trapped between an old timer and a newbie.

"I reckon you might have heard me ramble on before but I love a good tale. Anyway, here I go again," said Joshua. "Just like an alcoholic. Love to hear myself speak. Love to add two cups of detergent when I'm supposed to put just one in the old washing machine. Thank God for AA. Thank God for AA. Thank God for AA. Let me tell you something. Thank God for AA," said Joshua.

The AAs were hysterical. Even the newbie, a stupid kid with glasses, no more than eighteen years old, still shaking from DT's burst into laughter.

Joshua stared at the newbie and said, "Young newcomer you stick around these rooms. Get your ass to a sponsor. Work the steps. Get a sponsor. You earned your seat here."

"Okay," said the shaking newbie.

"Talk to me after the meeting. I will give you my number," said Joshua. Then he addressed the room and said, "Any other guys here willing to sponsor the newcomer?"

The newbie needs to go to fucking detox, thought Alethea.

Suddenly, she was angry. Tripping over the newbie, who was shaking even worse than before, Alethea got up and dumped her coffee in a sink behind the bar.

"Rude to get up during a meeting," said Joshua.

Alethea gave him the finger, and ran out of that hall as fast as she could. Huddling inside her jacket, she roamed around the parking lot that was full of cars from a Jaguar to an old Chevette. In the distance, she saw a homeless man walking his skuffy terrier. Sighing, she lit a cigarette. Even though people surrounded her, she felt very depressed and alone. Should she call her sponsor, Maude? It was around 8:00 pm. Maude was probably sitting in her bed, sipping a glass of warm milk and reading her Big Book, because as she shared frequently at meetings, reading the Big Book worked wonders for her insomnia. Even though Maude said that Alethea could call her anytime, Alethea did not have the heart to disrupt Maude's Big Book bedtime ritual.

Should she call her therapist at that clinic she went to? Hell, it was after hours, and the clinic's voicemail would refer her to the crisis hotline, and the last thing she needed were volunteers asking her if she wanted to commit suicide.

Should she go home, grab the dogs and go for a run along the deserted trails that were adjacent to her cheap mobile home? Maybe running was not a good idea, because it was evening, but if she ran with her two bloodhounds Cupid and Psyche, who in God's name would bother her? Bu then again bloodhounds were not exactly the smartest dogs on the planet. Well if the bloodhounds couldn't save her ass, she did have another option. As a firm believer in exercising her second amendment rights, she carried a micro 9mm SIG Sauer 365 in her fanny pack when she ran. It was a bit crazy doing so, especially if the gun went off and shot her, but she liked to go the extra mile when it came to safety.

Her dread grew as she drove back home on the 14. It was a weird feeling, this horrible dread, as hideous as that disgusting AA coffee. Why the hell did she drink that damn coffee? Why couldn't she just have gone to Starbucks and gotten coffee before that damn meeting? Or even better yet, why the hell did she even go that meeting? It was always the same. Some stupid moron would share his or her story and it was a variation of the same theme. And this time the moron's name was Joshua, of all things.

Living in the Mojave exacerbated her depression. And her paranoia was worsening by the hour. Besides seeing a therapist, going to meetings, running with a 9mm in her fanny pack, attending group therapy, working with a sponsor, and seeing a psychiatric nurse practitioner who prescribed her more medications than the ingredients found in a Long Island Iced Tea, the Joshua Trees freaked her out. Besides panic attacks, she had nightmares that the Joshua Trees had turned into zombies and were chasing her in the desert.

A few days later, she met Maude at Starbucks to do step study, which really bored the hell out of her, but she did it anyway. While Althea smoked, and gulped Café Americano down her throat as if the coffee was Drano unclogging a pipe, she watched Maude sip her decaf.

Who the hell drinks decaf? Alethea thought.

"I hate those trees," she said. "I truly hate them. They look defeated."

"Put Joshua Trees on your fourth step," said Maude. "Oh, and put both of your exes on the list."

Since she got sober five years ago, Alethea was writing up another fourth step inventory. That was because Maude was her fourth sponsor.

"I hate my exes," Alethea said.

"Exactly. That's why you put them on your list. Resentment is our number one offender," said Maude. "And lets meet again in a week, same time, same place. Start writing that inventory and keep going to meetings."

After she put Joshua Trees on the first column of her fourth step inventory, she decided to google Yucca Brevifolia to discover more about the mysterious species.

"Yucca Brevifolia, or Joshua Trees are indigenous to the Mojave desert. The Mormon settlers named them Joshua Trees because the shape of the trees was reminiscent of a story in the Old Testament where the prophet Joshua reaches his hands up to God in supplication."

Walking over to the window, she took a good hard look at the Yucca Brevifolias outside her house. She tried to imagine them as old holy prophets, but instead, they looked like an FBI swat team ready to break down the door.

One particular tree had many crooked branches, looming out of its trunk. That tree reminded her of Medusa, the Gorgon from Greek mythology, who had breathing snakes growing out of her head. If a poor soul gazed at Medusa, he was turned to stone.

Another yucca had two solitary branches, growing out of either side of its trunk. Like other yuccas, it was top heavy, so the effect was a bit comical. The poor yucca was in search of a head, kind of like the headless horseman in *The Legend of Sleep Hollow*.

Cupid and Psyche howled, almost in unison and Alethea snapped out of her reverie.

A few days after she saw Maude, Alethea sat in the Mojave Desert Community Clinic's waiting room anticipating her monthly tele-psychiatric consultation. She prayed that the TV shrink would prescribe Xanax for her anxiety. As long as she took the Xanax as prescribed, she could maintain her sobriety. While she sat in the waiting room, she thought about her stupid job as a blogger for an online recovery magazine. Writing for that stupid website made her eyes so tired, that she had no energy to finish her memoir, *Why Wasn't I named Jane*? While she adored Cupid and Psyche more than anything, sometimes it was hard to live alone.

Maybe that's why she was starting to believe that the trees beckoned to her at night, like the Sirens that sang to Odysseus when he made his 20-year journey to return home to Greece from Troy. She was way too isolated in the Mojave Desert.

Finally, a nurse opened a door, holding her chart and giving her a broad smile, as if seeing Alethea for her monthly consultation was the highlight of her year. "Nice to see you! Come on in."

Alethea dutifully followed the nurse down a corridor, which lead to a room that had one folding chair, an empty desk and a large flat screen TV which depicted Dr. Chiu, dressed in black, leaning over a desk, typing on his computer keyboard and staring at the screen. He ignored her.

"Dr. Chiu will be with you in a minute," said the nurse. As the nurse shut the door behind her, Alethea became claustrophobic. There were no windows inside the room. Suddenly, she smelled sweat. How could that be possible, unless she smelled her own sweat? Was she actually nervous? Well, of course she was. Her anxiety was cranking up and oozing out of her pores. Maybe that was a good thing. The doctor would see how nervous she was, and naturally, prescribe Xanax.

Finally, the voice from the TV spoke.

"How are you?" Chiu asked.

Dr. Melvin Chiu, of Long Beach, California stared directly at her, Ms. Alethea Papapapadaopulos formerly of the Bronx, New York, followed by Los Angeles, California, and God help her, followed by Mojave, California.

In order for Chiu to see her face-to-face, she had to gaze into the camera lens, which was directly under the flat screen. Instead, she stared directly at the wall behind the TV, so that Chiu could only see the whites of her eyes. She wanted to look insane, so that she could get the Xanax.

"I have nightmares," she said.

"What kind of nightmares?"

"I am being attacked by Joshua trees that have transformed into Medusa and the headless horsemen from *The Legend of Sleeping Hollow*."

She burst into tears.

Chiu pointed to a box of tissues that were on the desk.

"God bless you!" said Alethea, as she grabbed a fistful of tissues.

Perhaps Chiu could give her the right cocktail. Then all she had to do was pop a pill or two in the evening. A sense of serenity would allow her to focus writing, *Why wasn't I Named Jane?*

Chiu peered at Alethea's file on the TV screen, before looking up. "How are you doing on the Lamictal?" he asked.

"Okay, I guess," she said. "Why did you prescribe that to me again?"

"Bipolar disorder," he said. "And what about the other medication?"

"Everything seems to work," she said. "Except

I get panic attacks every day. Especially when I see those trees."

"I can prescribe Latuda," he said.

Shit. What the hell was Latuda? It sounded like a Japanese car.

"Latuda?" she asked.

"It's for a diagnosis that I like to call pre-psychotic anxiety. It takes the edge off."

"It sounds scary," said Alethea. "How about Xanax?"

He looked at the computer. "Well, says here you are a recovering alcoholic. I don't like to prescribe benzodiazepines to addicts."

"I won't get addicted, I promise," she said.

"Have you tried yoga? Or I can prescribe buspar. That helps with anxiety."

"I think Xanax is better," she said.

"Who's the doctor?" he said, with a grin. "Try the yoga. It works wonders."

Oh go to hell, Melvin Chiu of Long Beach, California. I am sure you live in a fucking mansion with a wife that goes to the salon every two weeks, gets Swedish massages, mud facials, manicures, pedicures and goddamn Botox injections. Oh and lets not forget the facelift and silicone implants. And by the way Chiu, you look like you had a hair implant and a nose job. God, I hate your guts.

After Alethea left her appointment, she drove to Wal-Mart on Avenue J in Lancaster, because there was no Wal-Mart in the goddamn desert. After she picked up her medication at the pharmacy, she went to the nursery section where she found a sickly bougainvillea in the clearance section. A few tears trickled down her cheeks. Was I actually married once? Or was it twice? After she put the plant in her cart, she walked around the store in a stupor. *Even though I am deteriorating, I will heal this plant*, she thought. Then, she stumbled over to the electronics section where she found a *Hatha & Flow Yoga for Beginners* DVD in the clearance bin.

She did not have a yoga mat, but she figured that the carpet, which was in desperate need of shampooing, would work.

A longhaired Hawaiian man named Yogi Kulani grinned at her from the TV.

"Yoga is the source of life," he said.

"Give me a break," she muttered.

"Let us begin," he said.

Alethea could barely follow his movements because Psyche had plopped on the carpet right next to her, while Cupid snored from the cheap leather couch that she had bought from Goodwill.

When Yogi Kulani got into the plough position, not only did she feel a dog's rubber duckie toy under her back, but as she pulled her legs over her head, she landed on Psyche. The rubber duckie dog toy squeaked.

As if on cue, Cupid jumped off the couch, and put his uge paw on her head. Then, he howled. As is if on cue, Psyche howled too.

"Get off," she said, pushing him away.

"Relax and breathe," said Yogi Kulani.

Cupid would not budge.

She pushed the dog away again.

"Relax and breathe," said Yogi Kulani.

Thankfully, Cupid went back to the couch.

She breathed.

The carpet had a weird odor. Several months ago, she purchased a Hoover Steam Vac carpet cleaner from Amazon on Black Friday, for half the price. The damn thing was still in the box.

"Fellow yogi's, breathe in through the nose, and make a sound when exhaling."

She could not move!

Her legs were trapped over her head!

She took a deep breath, and clumsily swung her legs back on the floor. Slowly, she got up, feeling like a broken marionette puppet.

Eyes shut, Yogi Kulani stood proudly. He had a stupid grin on his face. She watched in horror, as he lifted his arms in prayer towards the heavens.

Just like the yucca brevifolia.

While he brought the palms of his hands to meet in front of his heart, he said, "I see the spirit within you. Namaste." he said.

The video ended.

Squinting, she rubbed her neck, and reached for her cigarettes. Her heart pounded like an electrocuted rat bashing its head against a cage.

As she smoked, she felt a sharp pang across her chest. Wasn't yoga supposed to help her instead of kill her?

Outside the window, a yucca brevifolia sneered at her, as if to say, DON'T WORRY! I WILL PRAY FOR YOU!

An hour later, she found herself hooked up to an EKG at the ER at Tehachapi State Hospital. Because she had screamed that she was having a heart attack when she ran into the emergency room, the doctors saw her right away.

Bleeeep! Bleeep!

The intern was silent, as the machine recorded the electrical activity of her heart.

"What are you hiding from me?" she asked.

He did not respond.

"Please tell me. I live alone with my dogs. If something happens to me, animal control will take my dogs."

"Calm down," the intern said.

"How can you ask me to calm down?"

"Just breathe," the intern said. "You're making the EKG go faster."

She breathed, and then started coughing.

"Do you smoke?"

"Yes," she said. "Is that a problem?"

After what seemed to be an hour, he said,

"Your heart is perfectly fine. We can run more tests, but I believe you had an anxiety attack."

"No, forget the tests," she said. "I will take your word for it."

"I am going to write out a prescription for Xanax. Follow the directions carefully," he said.

"I will," she said.

By the time she got home, armed with a bottle of thirty Xanax pills, two refills, *Take as Needed*, it was about 10 am.

After she parked her SUV in front of the house, she ran over to the Medusa tree.

A neighbor, who was driving by, saw an anorectic looking woman in front of a Joshua tree stretching her arms up to the sky. What the hell? He put the car in PARK. Just as he was going to hop out of the car, to see if she was okay, he saw two large Bloodhounds howling at him from the window.

She saw him, flashing a maniacal grin.

"Namaste!" She yelled.

Startled, he put the car in reverse, drove backwards, and crashed, right into a Joshua tree.

Angie

It was drizzling in Lake Isabella. Angie sat on a broken step that was covered with a filthy brown carpet by the side of her cheap blue mobile home, and stared at the old metal shed that rose up in her yard like a wart. Behind the shed, were ten fir trees that were perpendicular to a cheap-gated fence that separated her shoddy mobile rental from Amerigas Propane Company. There was an array of propane tanks that looked like nuclear missiles, in the Amerigas parking lot.

Except for her Seiji, her Doberman, she lived a fairly reclusive life. She told herself that she was okay with that.

After she moved up here with Seiji, the red flag that she felt when she first saw the place became as crimson as a luminous red nova. While she unloaded her personal belongings, and dragged them into the house, neighbors emerged from their cheap mobile houses, like cockroaches coming out of a piece of rotten wood. They watched as she struggled with a hand truck, moving boxes, tables, and a television set. When she dragged her old mattress into the house, she heard a neighbor snicker. Naturally, none of the neighbors offered to help, but she did not want their help anyway.

A few days later, she reluctantly returned a U-Haul trailer to the U-Haul center next to Amerigas. Returning the trailer confirmed the fact that she was stuck up here in Lake Isabella. She had moved here because not only was the rent cheap, but also the landlady who lived in Reno allowed her to bring her beloved Seiji. Most landlords hated renting to tenants with breed restricted dogs, claiming that the dogs were a liability. As long she got renter's insurance, the landlady would let her rent the place.

Angie did not bother buying the renter's insurance.

And the landlady seemed to forget about it, too.

Seiji was inside the bedroom, snoring away on the mattress, which was on the floor. There was a hole in the roof of the shed. The rain poured. Angie lifted her face towards the sky as if she was receiving communion from a priest. By the shed, was an old, broken down Jacuzzi that was enclosed inside a cheap green metal siding. On the hot tub cover were the words, FUCK OFF painted in red. Part of the siding was torn, and a harsh wind caused it to flap back and forth, like the wet rag her ex fiancé used in lieu of an alarm clock, so that he could get her out of bed in the morning. Every morning at 6:45 am he would slap her face with the drenched rag while she slept on that awful cheap futon they owned. He slept on the couch. He did this because she had to earn her keep, and get to work, at the local diner in Palmdale, which was a few miles away from the ugly town of Lake Los Angeles where they lived at the time.

Back then her drinking was out of control. He drank too, but he always told her that he did not have a problem. Angie was the drunk. He could handle his liquor.

One day, he told her that he was going to Santa Fe to work on a film. He was a transportation coordinator, and travelled a lot. He never came back. That was over ten years ago. Angie had not dated since.

A few weeks ago, inside the shed, Angie came upon an old photo album that was covered with stains from motor oil, mud and rain. Most of the photos were removed from the plastic sleeves. While Angie skimmed through the pages, her fingers became covered with grime. Then, she came upon a grimy photo of an anorectic woman dressed in a cheap bridal gown. The bride looked dejected. Who would be morose on her wedding day? Next to her was a man in an inexpensive suit. There was a bright blue carnation on his lapel. The bride held a bouquet of white lilies. His arms were wrapped around her like a python suffocating a mouse.

Angie slammed the photo album shut. She ran out of the shed, turned on the hose, and ran her hands under the water. As hard as she tried, she could not remove the grime. She felt like Lady MacBeth.

"Hey, you!"

Her neighbor, Wilma shook her fist at Angie over the gate link fence that separated her house from Angie's.

With a sense of dread, Angie slowly walked over. Wilma wore a tacky red T-shirt with white lettering. *Make Fishing Great Again.* She wore brown shorts that were two sizes small and fuzzy pink Dora the Explorer slippers. The old lady smoked a cigarette in one hand, and held a mug full of steaming hot black coffee with the other. Her white hair looked electrocuted, as if she had touched a chewed up extension cord, and had gotten zapped. Wilma's eyes were as dark as black tar heroin.

"How are you?" asked Angie, even though she did not give a shit about Wilma's well being.

Sneering, Wilma took a long drag from her cigarette. As she exhaled, smoke came out of her nostrils, making her look like a dragon. Besides that, she was toothless, reminding Angie of Dunkleosteus, an extinct fish.

Extinct fish and dragon, thought Angie. What a wonderful combination.

"Dummy!" said Wilma, rapidly. She spoke as if she were on meth. "Just like the floozy who was in your house for you came running here, like a bat out of hell. If I was you, I'd fix to gets away fast as I can. There's some bad spirits here."

Angie did not respond. What could she say to the old coot anyway? Silently, she eyed the old lady's manufactured house that had dead tomato plants propped in windowsills which resembled white foam hinged hot dog containers. The yard was strewn with weeds, chopped wood, over packed garbage bags bursting and smelling like rotten cantaloupes, an old WANG computer monitor, and a decapitated Cupid birdbath. There was something dark, furry and smelly inside the bath.

"There's a dead rat in there, Wilma," Angie said.

"If I was you, I'd grab that mutt and runs outta here," Wilma said before she went back into her house, and slammed the door.

Inside the bathroom of her house, Angie gaped at her reflection. Even though she got food stamps, she hardly ate. She was as emaciated as the bride with the sad eyes. Suddenly, the usual depression swooped over like a tsunami. She stumbled from the bathroom to the bedroom. Angie crashed on the mattress next to Seiji who stared at her with a worried look. After she fell asleep, she dreamt that Wilma was chasing her down the streets of Lake Isabella with a dead rat, screaming, "get out!"

When she got up, it was about 3 am. She brewed a pot of coffee, and poured a cup in her New York mug, which was the only memento that she had of her hometown.

Angie still had nightmares about him and often woke up in the middle of the night in a cold sweat, imagining that he hovered over her, flapping the wet rag, while she slept. After he dumped her, she went to domestic violence groups, where she met Farahnoush, a young Muslim woman who shared a story about her abusive husband. "Imam kept telling me I was crazy. After a while, I started going crazy. And he took my son away and then I lost my mind to the point of where I ended up in the psych ward for a month. And naturally, Imam got custody. You know what's crazy? My name means joy. What kind of joke is Allah playing on me?"

A few months later, after the group ended, Angie read a New York Times article, which focused on women who had dishonored their families in the Middle East. She saw a picture of Farahnoush. The men in her family had tricked her into going back to their village in Afghanistan, and shortly afterwards, her brothers, along with her father, and most of the men in the village, murdered her with a wet pillowcase while she slept. According to Farahnoush's family, the young woman had disgraced her family, by leaving her husband and her son. Besides a profile photo, which depicted Farzani with her hajib, which she had not worn in the United States, there was a photo of the young woman's body being carried by her brothers. She was wrapped in a white shroud. There was also a picture of her hysterical mother who had nothing to do with her daughter's death.

The father deemed her murder to be an honor killing.

Wilma was outside, wearing a raincoat and holding an umbrella over a bonfire. Clutching a beer, the old woman stared into the flames, like the goddess Hestia who tended the hearth. As she walked across the yard, Angie stumbled, but caught her balance just in the nick of time. As usual, Angie was drunk. Hands trembling, she lit a cigarette.

"Do you have an extra cigarette?" Wilma asked.

Angie handed Wilma a cigarette over the fence.

"Drove Jessie nuts when I bummed cigs from her. Gave me a nasty look every time she hand me a cig over the fence. Same spot you standing in too," said Wilma. "I told her, I's your mom. Show some respect, girl!"

"Your daughter lived in my house?"

"Always tolds her to get out of that shithole. She caught him cheatin' on her, with some younger piece of ass that he treats like her shit don't stink. Treats my gal Jessie like she was the toilet paper that he wiped his goddamn fat ass. One's night, she waits like a hunter trackin' a buck til he pulls into the carport. Her car was right there, right in front of his fucking pick up truck. Girl, you see how narrow that carport is. Jessie had it all planned out, real good. That motherfucker park so close to the wall, and real close up to Jessie's van. She was waitin' inside, as still as my dead ex husband. Before that fat fool gets out of the van, she starts up the van. Stupid ass gets trapped between Jessie's back bumper and his hood. Jessie puts the car in reverse, then drive, then reverse." Wilma took a long puff from her cigarette before she burst into song. "*Your cheatin' heart, Will make you weep, you'll cry and cry, and try to sleep.* Goddamn it girl he sleep real good after that. She ask me, Mom can you find my old dried up bridal bouquet? Lilies. Not roses. Lilies for the dead. He bought 'em, too, that motherfucker. Ended up being on top of his grave."

She cackled.

Angie stared at Wilma in horror.

"Roadkill by the time the paramedics showed up."

"What happened to Jessie?"

"None of ya business, Miss nosy posey."

Still smoking the cigarette and clutching her beer, she walked back into the house.

Angie's photos were all packed inside a plastic bin. She skimmed through a pile, and found a photo of her and Jake in a Mormon cemetery. They were on a filming location, in Provo, and she, along with Clay, were working on a movie, *In the Arms of Joseph Smith.* He was the transportation coordinator. She was a driver. He sat around all day on one of those cheap mesh chairs that he bought from Wal-Mart for ten bucks. While he bossed the transportation crew around like King Henry the VIII, she drove actors around all day, in a large white van, from their hotels to the movie set.

Inside the photo they were in a cemetery strewn with tombstones. They stood next to each other, with tense smiles on their faces. His arms were folded in front of his chest, and her hands covered her crotch. Behind them, was a huge tombstone depicting a photograph of a young woman with wings, raising her arms in supplication to Joseph Smith who reaced reaching his arms out. The girl was ghostly. Joseph Smith was grinning, as if he were welcoming Angela to a Halloween party. The tombstone read, *Angela Moore, 1985-2004. Beloved Daughter. Why? Why?*

The film was about the tragic murder of a young Mormon woman named Angela Moore. Her Mormon husband shot her as she slept, and then blew his brains out. Clay thought it would be cool if they posed in front of the tombstone because the dead girl was named Angela.

A production assistant hurriedly snapped the photo, which turned out overexposed. There was a large sunspot on Angie's face.

That was the only photo of Angie and Clay during the five years that they had been together.

The next morning, after that photo was taken, she got up early at the Days Inn where they were staying. While he got to sleep in, she had to pick up some actors from their hotel, and take them to their latest filming location, the exterior of a gaudy Mormon Church. Jake was still asleep, probably hung over from another night of their getting sloshed on Jack Daniels and wine. After she got dressed, she went through his wallet. He always took her weekly check, and kept her on a strict allowance. Naturally, he had cashed her check. Inside the wallet, were ten one hundred dollar bills. She took the entire one thousand dollars because that was the amount that she should have been paid that week. Not one penny less, and not one penny more.

Back pay for just one week, you motherfucker, she thought. Let you off easy.

After she slung a duffel bag full of her clothing, the van's key, and her purse over her shoulder, she grabbed the ice bucket from the round hotel table. Overnight, the ice had melted, yet the water was frozen cold. She opened the door so she could bolt out of there, before he could grab her. Then, she walked over to the bed, and threw the bucket of water on his face.

"Ay yo, motherfucker!" She said, just like Bruce Willis in *Diehard.* Screaming, he stumbled out of bed, and crashed onto the floor. By then, she was running down the corridor, pressed the elevator button and as if by magic, the door immediately opened. Inside the lobby, there were members of the film crew who watched her with stunned looks on their faces, as she ran out of the hotel. Then, she located the van and drove back to Tujunga, where they lived in a remote cabin in the Los Angeles National Forest. The van belonged to the production assistant who took the photo. He did not press charges. Instead, he said, "One time I heard you screaming inside that room. Heard him say that you had to wear a bra. Then, I heard shattering noises like he was throwing bottles at you."

So why didn't you call the police? Angie thought. Or you had to mind your own business, right?

Inside the shed, she located the photo album. She slid the photo of her and Jake inside a grimy sleeve of a blank page. Drops of motor oil slipped through the sleeve, covering their faces. The tombstone glowed against the reflection of the moonlight that shone through a gaping hole in the shed's roof.

Screaming, she hurled the album where it bounced off the metal shed, and landed on top of a filthy couch.

Wilma was outside, smoking a cigarette. As Angie walked out of the shed, the old woman asked, "Heard some noise in there. You okay, girl? Don't see any men around here but you never knows."

A month later, Angie and Seiji moved out of the house. Angie took everything except for the photo of her and Jake, which was still inside the photo album on top of the filthy couch in the shed.

The Holy Face Medal

I park my old T-bird in front of Wendy's. Puffs of smoke pour out of my car, which coughs like it's in the final stage of COPD. A mechanic told me that I need a new catalytic converter, and there is no way in hell that my car is going to pass smog next year but that's 12 months away.

One day at a time.

I learned in AA that's how to deal with life.

I have to believe that, or else I will go crazy.

I also have to be of service to fellow alcoholics and addicts who are still suffering, or so my sponsor Mitch tells me. This whole crazy idea of my sponsoring this 40-year old rich ex housewife was his idea.

I walk by a row of cars, and spot Colleen's brand new white luxury Cadillac Escalade EXT crew cab.

I brace myself, and approach Starbucks, clutching my stupid Big Book, like a religious zealot clutching a Bible.

She sits outside on the patio. Her back is faced to me, and I can see her long blonde hair cascading over her shoulders. Colleen is a dowdy, plump woman, and yet somehow she manages to get all the guys in AA to drool all over her. Maybe its because she is a newcomer or maybe its because she always wears tight little spaghetti dresses with hems that go way up over her knees, revealing suntanned legs. And she always wears sandals that show off a fresh new pedicure.

Today she looks like she is hanging out at a country club, waiting for a waiter to bring her a pina colada with a plastic cocktail umbrella propped in the glass.

There is no else sitting outside at this Starbucks, which thanks to globalization, looks like a thousand other Starbucks all around the world.

This particular Starbucks is located in the Antelope Valley desert. How the hell did I end up in the AV? Oh that's right, I moved up here in a blackout ten years ago, with a fiancé who walked out on me the day our electricity got shut off, due to nonpayment. Seems like he had some younger woman waiting for him, in some candle lit villa somewhere in Albuquerque.

Up ahead, a woman driving a black BMW is passing through the drive-through. She has sunglasses and dyed red hair. I hear the barista ask, over the speaker,

"Hello, welcome to Starbucks. What can I get started for you?" The woman's face scrunches up like a walnut and she bleats out of a grape lipstick colored mouth, "Caramel macchiato with low fat soy."

Colleen turns, as if she has sensed that I am standing behind her. Her face breaks out into a wide grin, and her long teeth are as white as her new truck. Her lip-gloss shines, and she has makeup on, highlighting her big blue eyes. Today she boasts a bright red pedicure, and matching manicure. She wears a short blue dress that has pink hyacinth and blue bird prints. Around her neck, she wears a gold medal, hanging from a thick gold chain.

"Hi," she says, and gets up to give me a crushing hug. I smell perfume, shampoo and wine. The medal catches onto my knit blouse, and for a moment Colleen and I become Siamese Twins, connected at the chest.

"I am sorry," she laughs, and then bumps her forehead against mine, like we are two bulls in a rodeo.

"I am sorry!" she says, again.

"Stop moving, I got it," I say.

I disentangle the pendant, and get a good look. It's a holy face medal, showing an image of Christ on the shroud of Turin. Honestly, Christ's face reminds me of a 19th century post-mortem photograph.

Finally, I am free of Colleen and her medal. She collapses on a chair and guffaws, like a shopping mall Santa Claus.

I stare down at the table. She has a brand new copy of the Big Book, a notebook, pens, the 12 and 12, and a compass. Why the hell does she have a compass? Does she think that we are going to be drawing circles and studying Euclidean geometry? She also has a pack of Marlboro Lights, that she has not opened, and a brand new green lighter.

"I bought a pack of my own cigarettes," she says. "This way I don't have to keep bumming off yours."

Does she really smell of booze or am I just imagining things? Should I say something or just let her admit the truth to me? What the hell do I do?

"This morning I got a 30-day chip," she says, and pulls it out of a Michael Kors handbag.

I want to call her bluff, but I don't.

She is too excited about the damn white chip that is hanging off her key chain, which includes the Cadillac's keys. When I see the Cadillac's remote, a pang of envy shoots through my body like the pain from sciatica.

"Would you like a coffee?" I notice that she has not ordered, and I figure that hey, I should be nice and get her something. Besides, maybe the coffee will sober her up.

"I would love a hibiscus iced tea." She reaches for her bag again.

"It's okay, I got it," I said, and walk inside the Starbucks. Suddenly, I feel like running back to my crappy old T bird, and driving off, letting white exhaust pollute the air. The Native Americans used smoke signals for communication. Three puffs mean something is wrong. Maybe if my stupid car emits three puffs of white smoke, the universe will reach out and help me.

An hour later, after I have drunk two iced Americanos, and I watch Colleen chain smoke her Marlboros and chomp on the melting ice cubes from her pink colored iced tea, I have heard so much about her life. We have done everything except talk about the steps, which honestly seems like a moot point. How can I take her through the steps if she is drinking? She got a DUI six months ago, which is why she is in AA. Some judge in Santa Clarita mandated her to go to 12-step meetings, but she was able to get her license back, since it was a first time offense. She is newly divorced, and just moved back home with her mother. During the week, her daughters live with her ex, because of the DUI, but she has the girls on the weekends. Then, she tells me she works for the FBI and that she walks around with a Glock 43.

"Where's the gun?" I ask.

"It's on my upper thigh," she says.

I peek at the hem of her bird and flower-covered dress, which is way above her thigh, revealing too much skin and nothing that looks like a weapon.

"Listen, don't tell anybody else I work for the FBI. That's classified information."

"I won't tell a soul," I say.

I stare at the medal around her neck.

"That's very pretty," I lie. The medal gives me the creeps.

"My mom gave it to me, when I moved back home. I'm Catholic."

"I am Greek Orthodox," I say. "But right now I like to think of myself as spiritual."

Colleen nervously lights a cigarette and fingers her medal. I don't think she is listening.

"What do you think of Stan?" she asks.

"Stan?"

"From AA. Blonde Stan," she says.

"He is a nice guy. He used to date my friend Amanda," I say.

"She died," Colleen says.

"Yes, she hit her head on a coffee table one night in her living room and fell over dead. They think it was a stroke. She just lived alone with her cat."

"Stan misses her," Colleen says.

"Well, she was my hairdresser. Now I just go to Supercuts."

Colleen lights another cigarette and says, "He asked me out, I mean, Stan did."

"He is a nice guy," I say, and stare off into space.

I refrain from telling her that he had broken Amanda's heart, and had dumped her several months before she died. This is because she had started using again, and people in AA told him to leave her to fend for herself. After she died, Stan seemed interested in asking me out. One night, he wanted to have dinner, but I told him I was writing a PowerPoint presentation on Diane Arbus for a *History of Photography* class. At that time, I was working towards my Associates in photography, and I was a full-time student at Antelope Valley Community College.

Stan expressed interest in Arbus, so I sent him the presentation, which included many of her photos. He said her photography was way too weird, specifically the photo of the *Boy with the Hand Grenade*. He said that I looked like Arbus, with my short hair. After I told him Arbus killed herself and sometimes I entertained suicidal thoughts, but would not kill myself because I had too many pit bulls, and God only knew animal control would confiscate them if I croaked, he backed off.

I seem to have an unsettling effect on men.

Honestly, the thought of being in a relationship makes me feel numb. I'd rather be independent and pay my bills, and make sure the electricity is always on. I don't like the dark.

The next time we meet, she can't stop crying. It is a cool overcast day in October, and she wears a jean mini skirt and a tight white t-shirt. I have cowboy boots on and she wears sandals, revealing a black pedicure.

Her red fingernails are chipped, and she is not wearing the holy face medal.

"I am not drunk," she says. "But I don't know if I can do this. Work these steps. I don't believe in God. My mom and I had a big fight, because I lost the medal. I have no idea where it is. But I am not drunk."

I stare at her. She does not smell of booze or perfume.

"You don't have to believe in God to work the steps," I say. "Just a power greater than yourself."

"Does that mean I should collect crystals, and meditate in front of a Better Home and Gardens rock fountain?" she asks. "I have no idea what you are talking about! Besides, I'm Catholic!"

"Well the truth is I have a hard time wrapping my mind around a higher power. Being Greek Orthodox has really installed the idea of a Jesus who looks like a terrorist, ok? When I first got sober, I took an astronomy class, and just knowing that the galaxy was eternal made me visualize something greater than myself. Anyway, surrendering to a higher power is in the third step. We have time to talk about that. But lets work on step one," I say.

"Ok," she says.

After she admits that she is powerless over alcohol, and that her life is a total mess, I ask, "What's this whole thing with the FBI?"

"I am a school teacher," she says. "Working for the FBI sounds better, don't you think? The truth is, I don't even own a gun."

We look at each other and laugh.

"I have something for you. You said you were studying photography, so maybe you can use this," she says.

She hands me a bulky camera bag.

"It was my father's," she says. "He's been gone for almost 20 years."

I zip open the bag, and there is a Minolta film X-570 SLR, along with a huge telephoto lens, inside a black tube and a few other lenses, and a flash. Everything is so neatly arranged, and the camera has a brand new strap.

"I know it was a long time ago, but I miss him."

She looks up at me. Her eyes are full of tears.

"It feels like yesterday that he died. Anyway, I found the camera. It's yours."

A few days later, I see her at the Palmdale hall. She is outside, while the meeting is going on. Stan and a few other men circle her. I walk towards the hall, and she sees me. She breaks out into a large grin. As usual, she wears a little mini skirt. I look terrible. She has a fresh new manicure, and her high-heeled sandals reveal an equally fresh pedicure. I look at my hands. There are remnants of duct tape and dirt underneath my nails. This morning I was served with a three-day notice, which I ripped off my gate like a crazed animal. I didn't want the neighbors to see it. The papers were taped with duct tape all over the gate. Even though I have washed my hands ten times this morning, scrubbing them over and over like Lady Macbeth trying to rub blood off her hands, they still feel dirty.

A month ago, I had a job an hour away in Lake Hughes, where I worked as a kennel assistant at a dog rescue. And then I started having serious problems with my car, and a local mechanic warned me not to drive long distance. I couldn't get to work because this place was miles away and so I got fired, and couldn't pay my rent this month.

Colleen hugs me. I smell the booze, and I flinch.

"Stan and I went on a date. He is so wonderful! I love you!"

"Ditto," I say.

During the break, I pull Stan aside, and I said, "Is she drinking again?"

He nervously combs his fingers through his long brown hair. Stan is tall, and looks like George Washington without wooden teeth.

"That's her choice. All I can do is take her to meetings, and maybe she will catch on. When I was with Amanda, too many people had too much to say, and I was stupid to listen."

His face turns red, from anger or from guilt, I can't tell.

"It's your life, Stan."

"Thanks for being her sponsor, " he said.

Her sponsor? The way he said that made me feel like I was some kind of hospice nurse, and Colleen was my terminally ill patient.

The next time, we are supposed to meet, she is there, waiting for me at Starbucks, and I have overslept and I have stood her up. It's two in the afternoon, and I huddle under the covers, shaking. I was served with an unlawful detainer the day before. That means I have to go to court and respond within five days, or else my dogs and I will be out in the streets. And today is the second day and I haven't done jack shit.

Prior to meeting Colleen, I had planned to be at the darkroom at the college, where this semester I am taking one film photo class because that is all I can afford. Over the weekend, I had used the Minolta, and had taken some black and white shots of a Joshua tree. It was a simple depth of field assignment. I shot the same damn tree on different F-stops. In one pocket of the camera bag, I found a Fuji color roll that had been shot yet not developed. It probably belonged to Colleens' dad, and he never got a chance to develop it.

I mean to call Colleen but I fall asleep again, and I am walking through the desert. The sky is yellow, the way I imagine Hiroshima to have been after the Atomic bomb. There is a man up ahead, wearing a white robe and sandals. He kneels down and prays. Up ahead is Colleen, and she has a Polaroid camera. She takes a picture of the man. Then she hurls the photo on the desert ground, and I run and pick the print up. I wait for an image to develop and I hear her up ahead laughing and I can't see the man anymore, he is gone.

Close by I see a rattlesnake. Colleen yells out, "How did you find me here?"

The snake has approached me, and if I get up, it will bite. An image develops on the print, and before I see it, I hear, "How the hell did you find me?"

Colleen told me later that she had waited for me at Starbucks for two hours.

"There was this nutty red headed lady in a BMW. She was such a bitch," Colleen says. "She went through the drive through. After she ordered her stupid drink, it was a caramel macchiato with low fat soy. I mean what the hell is low fat soy? Isn't soy already low fat? Anyway, she told the guy that I was smoking on the patio, and didn't they have some new law that prohibited smoking on the patio?"

Colleen slurs her words.

"So I told the bitch to fuck off, and they threw me out of there. Guess we have to find another Starbucks."

"Colleen, you are still drinking."

"I had a slip," she says.

"I can't help you if you are still drinking."

"What are you telling me? You don't want to be my sponsor anymore?"

"No," I said. "I can't."

She bursts into tears, and wails like Andromache, when her child was thrown off the walls of Troy.

After I was evicted, my German Shepherd Hedda and I lived with a guy who I had met at an AA meeting years ago. He said he was sober, but I found empty bottles of Vodka hidden under piles of sweaty clothing and dirty socks in the living room. Thankfully, we had our own room, and Hedda safeguarded me from this guy, the way the Sphinx guarded the city of Thebes from travellers, unless they could solve her famous riddle. Hedda had no riddle, she just barked. We lasted there for a tortuous month, and then I found a small trailer up in the Mojave.

We have been here a year. The desert landscape that was in my dream surrounds me in real life. I wonder if the Mojave is purgatory, and I am paying for past transgressions.

Guilt compels me to call Colleen's cell. A Hispanic male picks up. He doesn't speak English. I suppose she has another cell phone number, but I have no idea how to find her. She is not on Facebook or any other social media sites. I connect the cell phone to a charger, and plug that into an electric outlet in the bathroom, which is as claustrophobic as an aircraft lavatory.

I feed Hedda, warm up a slice of pizza, and watch *House of Cards*. I am so tired, but I have to brush my teeth. Inside the bathroom, I notice that there is a text. It's from my sponsor, Mitch.

"Stan said last night at the meeting that they were supposed to take Colleen off life support yesterday at 4. She drank herself to death I guess."

The camera and the lens are all tucked away inside the bag, safe and sound. I find the Fuji color roll that belonged to Colleen's father. The next day, I drive down to Lancaster and drop the roll off at the one-hour photo department. I am not sure what I am hoping to find.

After I pick up the photos, I skim through them. Most of the prints are a brownish black, like mud after a rainy day. I find an overexposed print, and I see a grainy image of a man's face. His eyes are shut. Pope Benedict XVI once said, that in the shroud of Turin, we see a reflection of our sorrow in the suffering of Christ. Beneath the desolation, the man's face glows with tranquility, which is what I imagine for Colleen. Inside her coffin, which will shelter her like a cocoon made of metal, she will be sealed away forever, buried six feet under, but she will be safe, and protected from a world that only gave her torment. Perhaps the suffering that I see in this image is not Colleen's, but rather my own anguish.

For Shannon

Help Wanted: Live In Nanny. Free Room and Board. One West 72nd Street.

One West 72nd Street was a sight to behold. The black kings that were molded on the black gate, which encircled the fortress like building, made me shudder. Not only was the exterior of the notorious Dakota featured in the film, *Rosemary's Baby*, but also the building was the site of John Lennon's tragic assassination which happened only five years ago. Shaking dark thoughts aside, I walked up to the security booth, which was to the left of the building's archway.

"Can I help you?" asked the aging security guard, who looked like he had worked there since 1884, when the building was constructed.

"I have an appointment with Mrs. Schlagt," I said.

The guard sneered at my cheap blazer, and then stared at my skirt with disgust. Suddenly, I realized that the price tag was securely fastened with adhesive on the lower left hand corner of my skirt. The price, $6.99, was written in huge black magic marker. I had bought the outfit from a thrift store in the

Village. Nervously, I ran my hand through my hair, which was in desperate need of trimming.

"Name?" he finally asked.

"Lily Romano," I said, as I pushed away a strand of untrimmed hair away from my eyes.

He picked up a phone, dialed and mumbled a few words. After he hung up, he said, "Follow me."

As I yanked the tag off, which naturally left a blob of residue on the damn skirt, I followed him through the arched main entrance, where so many years ago, horse drawn carriages transporting gentlemen wearing coattails, and women in petticoats, entered. The face of the Dakota Indian, which hung over the entrance, stared straight ahead, a somber look on his face. We crossed the central courtyard where the carriages once disembarked travelers. We entered an old fashioned Turnbull Traction elevator, which was covered from floor to ceiling in red velvet. At the corner of the elevator, was a black mahogany bench.

"Is that an antique?" I asked, pointing at the bench.

In response, the guard slammed the elevator door shut. As the elevator left the ground floor, creaking and shivering as if the cables were about to break, I muttered a *Hail Mary* under my breath. The guard gave me a look of disgust, as if he had just discovered a hair in a bowl of spaghetti and meat sauce.

Before the elevator reached its destination, I heard the ticking. The guard stared ahead, a grim look on his face. Finally, the elevator stopped, and the door slowly opened. The ticking grew louder. After I emerged into the foyer, I heard the elevator door shut behind me, like a lid crashing on a coffin. A Hispanic maid silently waited for me. She gave me a solemn look as if she was a nun and I was a dead body at a wake. As I followed her down the hall, my mouth dropped open. As far as I could see, floor to ceiling, the penthouse was decorated with clocks of all types, and sizes. There were cuckoo clocks, alarm clocks, carriage clocks, balloon clocks, wall clocks, windup clocks and pendulum clocks. Every five seconds, an alarm blared. Every ten seconds, a cuckoo cuckooed. Every fifteen seconds, a Victorian-style grandfather clock resounded a reverberating dark gong or two that shook the apartment like a tsunami.

The clocks were not synchronized.

For a split second, I wanted to run out of that penthouse screaming, and take the subway back home, but then reality hit me.

Anyone would give their right arm to live in the Dakota! Especially someone like me who lived in Flatbush!

As I followed the maid, I stumbled over a Minnie Mouse clock.

This was not a normal Minnie. This was a Minnie Mouse that had an evil sneer on its face. This Minnie looked like the Bride of Chucky.

The maid stopped in front of a huge room and pointed, as if she were the Ghost of Christmas Yet To Come showing Ebenezer Scrooge impending doom. Silently, I walked inside a high ceilinged green and white walled living room, which featured an eclectic combination of Americana, Victorian and Louis the Fifteenth furniture. And then there were the clocks. On two walls were dolls' head clocks and lighthouse clocks. The other two walls were devoted to cuckoo clocks. In each corner of the room was a gothic grandfather clock. The Rococo display cabinet was crammed with mantel clocks, and an hourglass. On an Americana end table was an old French decimal clock from the time of the French Revolution. Out of the corner of my eye, I saw more clocks in the adjoining dining room. The sound of ticking crept under my skin, and made its way through my bloodstream and into my brain. Just when I was about to go into cardiac arrest, a cuckoo emerged from a clock, retreated, and emerged once again. After that cuckoo retreated, another cuckoo emerged from another clock. After that second cuckoo retreated, eight cuckoos emerged in unison. The time according to the cuckoo clocks was two, three and four pm. I felt as if I were seeing CATS on Broadway.

I was so hypnotized by the cuckoo clocks that I almost forgot why I was there to begin with. Behind me, I heard the sound of coughing.

Mrs. Nancy Schlagt, who looked like a young Mia Farrow, sat in a gaudy Victorian style chair. For a moment, I thought that I was on the set of *Rosemary's Baby*, and that Schlagt would lead me to a nursery where there was a black bassinet with a hanging upside down cross. Inside the bassinet, there was the Son of Satan, a cute little bugger with yellow eyes and claws.

"My sweet son of Satan!" Mrs. Schlagt would say. "This is your new nanny!"

A few gongs from a grandfather clock snapped me out of my reverie.

"You are on time," said Schlagt with a smile. While Schlagt donned a classic Chanel suit, she wore red patent leather shoes that were more apropos for a Raggedy Ann doll. On her left wrist, she wore five wristwatches, including a shiny Rolex.

I smiled.

She leaned back and said, "The precious ones are eating dinner."

Suddenly, two children, clutching forks, blasted through the room, screaming. When they saw me, they stopped in their tracks, staring at me as if I were the spinach hanging from their forks. The boy, whose face was covered with chocolate milk, wore a sailor outfit that would have been more appropriate for a toddler. The girl, who had linguini hanging from her long blonde hair, wore a tutu and pink ballerina slippers. Suddenly, they grinned at me. The two entities looked like evil gnomes from a *Grimm's Fairy Tale*. I would have preferred being a nanny for the Antichrist.

Once again, the damn cuckoo clocks began their bizarre sequence.

"Interesting clocks," I said.

The gnomes glared at me.

"Heirlooms. Absolute treasures. Like my children," Schlagt said. "I have been meaning to get a clock's man out here, but ah well! First things first!" As she stood up to greet me, with a Cheshire cat smile on her face, I cast a furtive glance at the girl who was attempting a ballet jump. The boy caught me staring at his sister, and threw his fork at me. While the fork narrowly missed me by a quarter of a centimeter, the utensil knocked over a sundial, which was perched on a coffee table. The sundial, covered with spinach, crashed onto the wood tiled floor.

Schlagt yelled loudly, masking the sound of the dancing cuckoos. "MARIA!"

Maria ran in. Carefully, she placed the sundial back on the coffee table. After she wiped it off, she bolted out of the room, but not before she cast me a look of pity. After she left, Schlagt said, pointing to a preschool plastic red chair, which was illustrated with SMURFS. "Please have a seat! Make yourself at home!"

I am petite, so I was able to squeeze into the chair. As Schlagt towered over me, I felt like I was about to be interrogated by the CIA.

"So my dearest Lily! Tell me a little bit about yourself. Why do you want to be a nanny?"

"A ninny!" laughed the girl, as she bent her knees in a pathetic effort to plié.

"My darling girl takes ballet downtown. Of course, you will take her to class. 4 pm, Mondays, Wednesdays, and Fridays, after you pick the children up from Dalton."

"And I take tai chi," said the boy.

He stood with his feet about a foot apart, transporting his hands in a cupped stance with his palms facing up. After he inhaled, he twisted his body, rotated his hands and exhaled.

"Yes, Tai Chi for my son. 4 pm. Mondays, Wednesdays and Fridays," said Schlagt. "Tai Chi is on the Upper East side. Ballet is in Soho."

"The classes are on opposite ends of Manhattan," I said, panicking.

"Ninny!" said the boy, as he continued his Tai Chi exercise.

"Ninny!" said the girl, as she pirouetted.

I wanted a Xanax.

While the boy stuck his tongue out at me, a few pendulum clocks struck out several gongs that ran through out the house. I felt like I was Psyche, being punished by the goddess Aphrodite who just happened to resemble Mia Farrow.

"The children require much care," she said, smiling. "They are at the delicate age when they are processing."

The boy grabbed a digital clock, and hurled it at his sister, missing her by a foot. She threw her fork at him. Then they looked at each other and screamed.

"Screaming, as introduced by Dr. Arthur Janov," said Schlagt. "Are you familiar with primal therapy?"

"Not really," I said.

"My mother was a close friend of Dr. Janov's. As a matter of fact, she introduced John and Yoko to him shortly after they moved into the Dakota. When I was a little girl, there was so much screaming going on inside these walls," said Schlagt. "So much wonderful primal screaming!"

She sighed, as if she were recollecting a trip to Maui.

A tall middle-aged man in a business outfit, holding a briefcase popped his head into the room. He wore a fedora hat. "When are you going to call someone to fix these goddamn clocks?" he said.

"This is my husband, Fred," Schlagt said. "Fred, meet Lily! She might be our new nanny! Fingers crossed!"

"Fingers crossed!" said the boy.

"Fingers crossed!" said the girl.

Screaming, they ran out of the room.

As a loud gong reverberated throughout the apartment, Fred Schlagt stared me, shaking his head.

"The last nanny jumped off the roof," he said.

Then he walked away.

Schlagt smiled brightly and said, "Tell me a bit about yourself. Why do you want to be a ninny?"

Before I could even open my mouth, the demons from hell returned. Startled, I looked up. As the evil boy hurled a pie in my direction, the girl broke into hysterical laughter. Suddenly, I felt whipped cream and chocolate all over my face. Cherry syrup covered my long hair. Ice cream dripped onto my outfit. As I stood up, the damn chair was fastened onto my butt.

The creatures laughed.

Nonplussed, Schlagt repeated, "Why do you want to be a ninny?"

With the plastic chair still attached to my derriere, I stumbled out of that cursed building, as if I were trying to find refuge from the San Andreas earthquake. I could hear the guard, along with several Upper West siders laughing. Blinded by chocolate and whipped cream, I toppled against the fence, and my damn panty hose got caught against one of those ridiculous black king artifacts. As I pulled away, I noticed a snag that was about a foot long. I didn't care. All I could focus on was getting to the subway, which was several feet away, on Central Park West. Even though my feet were killing me, thanks to the damn pumps, I stumbled towards my destination, almost knocking over a nanny pushing an ugly toddler, who looked like a Cabbage Patch doll, in a stroller, while she walked an ugly Giant Schnauzer. Even though I startled the trio, I did not stop to apologize. My mind was on one thing only. When I reached the subway, I felt the familiar hot air, which informed me that a train was on its way. Clutching the bannister, I stumbled down the stairs, like a drunken homeless person. As I heard the train screeching into the station, I jumped the turnstile, losing the Smurf chair. Behind me the woman in the booth yelled, but I ran towards the front of the platform, breathing in the stench of the rusty B train heading for Brooklyn. As the train doors opened, I darted inside. Out of breath, I plopped down next to a man with dreadlocks. He wore old baggy clothing, and his shoes had holes. Even though he smelled like he had not taken a shower for a week, I wanted to hug him. Other passengers looked up, some reading the New York Post or the Daily News, others snoring away, their heads resting against metallic seats. Except for a businessman who snickered at the sight of a woman covered with chocolate pie and whipped cream from head to foot, the other passengers gave me a quick lookover, and then went back to their business.

I was home.

About the Author

Sevasti Iyama has written for *The Fix, After Party*, the *Antelope Valley Press* and the *Kern Valley Sun*.

Several of her short stories have been published in Adelaide Literary Magazine, and she was a finalist for the Adelaide Voices Literary Contest 2018. The story that won was published in the *Adelaide Literary Award Anthology—Best of 2018.* While she studied acting and writing at NYU, she received her Bachelors from Southern New Hampshire University where she will acquire a Masters Degree in Creative Writing in February 2020. Additionally, her short story, *The Rottweiler* will be published in Badlands Literary Journal in 2020.

www.ingramcontent.com/pod-product-compliance
Lightning Source LLC
Chambersburg PA
CBHW020023030726
47499CB00007B/2237

* 9 7 8 1 9 5 1 8 9 6 3 3 1 *